Undercover Babymoon

by

Karina Bartow

*Unde(a)feated Detective Series,
Book Four*

Undercover Babymoon

Cover Art by *Teddi Black*

The Wild Rose Press, Inc.
PO Box 708
Adams Basin, NY 14410-0708
Visit us at www.thewildrosepress.com

Publishing History
First Edition, 2024
Trade Paperback ISBN 9781509257614
Digital ISBN 9781509257621

Unde(a)feated Detective Series, Book Four
Published in the United States of America

Dedication

To Uncle Gary & Aunt Nancy with love
Check YOU out!

Prologue

Detective Minka Avery closed the car door behind her and followed Cael, her partner and brother-in-law. The two trekked onto one of the trails that surrounded Lake Conway in the Belle Isle neighborhood of Orlando, Florida. She tucked her hands into her pockets as they approached the crime scene, not wanting anyone to note the perspiration on her palms. Despite her years in law enforcement, she'd never grown comfortable in the presence of a dead body and didn't aspire to be a homicide detective. Because of some shuffling around at the Orlando Police Department and a cold case she and Cael recently solved, though, they earned the so-called promotion.

As they neared the body, a distinct stench wafted to her very sensitive nose. Back in her days on foot patrol, she'd grown accustomed to the odor of decay, but a decade later, she'd lost her tolerance. She halted her steps a few feet short of their destination, hoping if she waited for a beat, her system would acclimate.

Cael pivoted in her direction once he realized her absence by his side. "Are you all right?"

She nodded, suppressing the urgent wish to heave hanging right there in her chest. "I'm just going to listen from here for now."

To her gratitude, her partner who was well acquainted with her weakness, didn't object. After he neared the corpse, medical examiner Sadie Grey began rattling off the facts that she and the other responding officers had already ascertained. She began her oral report but abruptly paused and peered over at Minka. "Can you hear me from there?"

The question humiliated Minka on several fronts. For one, she hated appearing pathetic and unprofessional. Besides that, she wondered if the woman fostered preconceived ideas about her deafness. She fought her urge to point out her cochlear implant. "Yes, don't worry about me. I'm getting used to the aroma, that's all."

"I understand, believe me. Even after three years on the job, it gets to me once in a while, too, especially now that I'm pregnant."

The woman's candid manner surprised Minka, given that Sadie didn't show at all so she couldn't be much farther along than her first trimester. She would've congratulated her, but the medical examiner segued right back into the briefing about the body, beginning with her estimation that the time of death occurred at least five days ago, which explained the foul horrendous odor.

The victim—a male named Rowan Matthews—appeared to have died by blunt force head trauma and lay in an isolated area where no one discovered him until a jogger found him during her morning run. The poor woman stood by her car with another officer, waiting to give her statement to Minka and Cael. Minka tried her best to focus on Sadie's account and padded a little bit closer when she highlighted a few details about the man's position. She regretted the brave move, with her already unsettled stomach tossing some more. To spare herself further embarrassment, she darted behind some trees before the nausea overtook her.

After her body cleansed itself—as her earthy sister-in-law termed it—she took a couple of paces toward the scene but hesitated when her phone vibrated with an incoming call. The instant she read the ID, she retreated behind another tree, in need of privacy once more.

After she greeted the caller, the lady replied, *"Hi, Mrs. Avery. This is Gwen from Dr. Bailey's office. She just wanted to let you know your lab results are in; they confirm your pregnancy. Congratulations!"*

A positive home test and every symptom which occurred during the past few weeks, including what just happened a few feet behind her, pointed to the basic facts, but Minka's heart still burst with jubilation. She and her husband, Wes, had yearned for a second child for years, and the long-awaited prospect bloomed inside her. *At last.* With tears welling up in her eyes, she thanked the receptionist and scheduled an appointment for her first pre-natal visit.

Afraid to tell anyone this early, she regained her composure and forged ahead. Cael met her halfway. He always displayed such warm empathy, but the intense expression on his face showed his irritation.

"What are we going to do about this, Minks? I know you hated to refuse the promotion to Homicide, but we won't make this work if you can't even make it through a briefing without losing your breakfast."

"Cael, give me a break. This is day one. I'll adjust after we get a couple more under our belts, just like when we were on patrol."

He glanced around, like he was checking for anyone who might overhear them. "But we aren't rookies anymore. This is humiliating."

3

"It is for me, too, but I promise I'll get better." As soon as she uttered the words, she recalled Sadie's admission about heightened senses. She shook her head, aware of what she had to do. "I'll probably have to buy nose plugs or something for the next seven months or so."

"Seven months?" He looked horrified. "That's it, I'm calling the captain."

She grabbed his arm to stop him. "Please, be patient. Sadie and I can work it out. After all, we're both smelling for two."

For a moment, Cael's eyes glazed over with confusion—until his face lit up. He embraced her, then joked, "What pairs better with a dead body than a new baby?"

Chapter One

Three Months Later

Minka lay on the exam table, soaking in the moment. Wes and their daughter, Caela, stood beside her, gazing at every movement of the newest addition to their family. They could make out the twenty-one-week-old fetus on the screen in greater detail than the one from Minka's first ultrasound. The vividness of the image blew Minka away. Meanwhile, the sister-to-be posed question after question, all of which were thankfully age-appropriate.

"Do you think the baby could come before November?" Caela asked the doctor. "Mommy's tummy is bigger than Sadie's, which is weird because Mommy caught the baby from her at work. Sadie's due in October, so could Mom beat her?"

The innocent seven-year-old still believed Minka contracted her pregnancy like a stomach bug from her close friend. Since her insightful daughter proved very sharp otherwise, suspecting her mom's condition long before they planned to tell her, Minka embraced Caela's naïve reasoning

Poker faced and treating the seven-year-old's question with the seriousness it deserved, Dr. Bailey explained, "She could, but your little sibling would be better off waiting. It's like keeping a bowl of popcorn in the microwave for the right amount of time so that you don't get any un-popped kernels. Sadie's baby is older and more developed than this one. Every mommy carries her baby differently."

"And our kids clamor for attention, like their father!" Minka nudged her husband while they held hands.

He kissed her head. "And their mother."

Caela accepted the logic, but her frown indicated her impatience over another five-month wait. Still, she giggled when her brother or sister's hand rose in a seeming wave. Fittingly, Dr. Bailey took the sensor off of Minka's stomach after that, making Caela groan. "I want to know if it's a boy or a girl."

"I'll tell you in the hallway when Mommy's getting dressed," the doctor told her, aware of Minka's desire not to learn her child's gender ahead of time. She shifted toward Minka. "You sure you're going to let them have this power over you?"

"I guess I am." She laughed, certain they'd be lording it over her for the next five months. "The wait would kill my husband even more than it would Caela."

Wes gave her a playful jab.

"Then, follow me, you two. Everything looks fantastic, Minka," Dr. Bailey said. "You're halfway there."

As the door closed, Minka wiped the sonogram gel off her skin and buttoned up her shirt. She tied the drawstring sewn into the blouse that encompassed her middle and accentuated its growth. She supposed her husband called it right when he teased her about liking attention when it pertained to the pregnancy. Considering her long journey back to motherhood, she took pride in showing off her little one's development…and the fact that more was happening than just weight gain.

She giggled at her daughter's squeals through the wall, as her active unborn child tossed inside her womb, probably hyped from the orange juice she'd guzzled while waiting to be called into the exam room for the ultrasound. Five months may have seemed like an eternity to Caela, but Minka and Wes hoped to have everything prepared in the short span. The nursery Wes and their friend's construction crew were adding above the garage still needed drywall, carpet, paint, and furniture. For as long as they tried to expand their family, they hadn't put much in place for the awaited event. She expected to be racing around right up until she entered the delivery room.

Minka hopped off of the table and grabbed her purse, in need of the restroom. As she washed up at the vanity, she ran her hands through her auburn hair to try to control the frizz. The June heat and its accompanying humidity always took its toll, and her excess hormones gave her natural waves even more volume. Once she regained control of it, she meandered into the lobby to book her next appointment.

All the while, her husband and daughter's knowing grins couldn't be tamed. They remained quiet on their stroll out of the office, until Caela, not surprisingly, was the one to crack. "You sure you don't want us to tell you, Mommy?"

"Yes, just like I won't the next fifty times you ask."

"But why?"

"Because I didn't even want to know you were a girl, but Daddy had surprised me enough for the whole year, and I needed some measure of sanity." She gave Wes a sidelong glance about his long ago stint in the witness protection program after his amateur sleuthing put him on the bad side of the mafia. "This time, I want that moment of surprise."

"It could be right now," Caela replied.

Her parents had to snicker. "But, then, you guys wouldn't have anything to hold over me. Your fun would be over."

The line of reasoning seemed to make the girl reconsider, silencing her for the rest of the ride home. Minka had requested the rest of Thursday afternoon off to enjoy her family, with just over an hour remaining on her shift. Given that Wes taught high school biology at the local School for the Deaf, he and Caela could spend their summer together. Minka cherished that they could soak up that father-daughter bonding, but she seized any opportunity she could to be a part of their time off.

Although she didn't have to go back to the precinct, she had some paperwork and emails to send, all in regard to her first homicide case. Rowan Matthews, the victim at the lake, had ties to a loan shark, whom she and Cael had apprehended, along with his fixer. As they anticipated, the duo was connected to a string of multiple crimes across the county and beyond, making it necessary to collaborate with several other departments. The two detectives had never conducted such a wide-reaching investigation.

Wes offered to barbecue their dinner, encouraging his wife to relax. She took his advice and napped for half an hour before Caela entreated her mom to push her on the swing of the backyard playset. In all truth, Caela could pump her feet and control the swing, but it'd always been a special activity shared between her and her parents.

Trying to satisfy her daughter's desire to soar higher without endangering either of them, Minka gazed over at the infant swing beside her. She fondly remembered the day Wes hung it up and her trepidation when she placed her five-month-old inside the seat the first time. At that age, Caela didn't laugh many times, but the tot giggled for the entire ride.

Once she outgrew it, the seat just rocked with the wind, unoccupied except for when they had tiny visitors. Minka's optimism that they'd use it again waned as the years passed without another baby entering their world. Despondent, she'd suggested Wes take it down the previous summer since Cael's son, Tyson, had grown too big for it. Her husband's procrastination worked to their advantage for a change, and she couldn't wait to start making memories out there with her two little ones by year's end.

After Wes finished prepping the grill, Caela hollered for him to take Minka's spot. The sweet girl claimed she didn't want to tire out her mother, but Minka gathered that her gentle force didn't suffice for the daring kiddo. Wes didn't disappoint, hurrying over to give her a couple of big heaves before she could fly high enough for him to run beneath her in his underdog trick.

Regardless of Caela's actual intentions to give her a break, the mother-to-be embraced it, in need of one. She retreated to the chaise lounge on the patio and switched on the nearby fan, content to play spectator. Right as her eyelids folded shut, her phone rang on the table beside her. To her relief, the call didn't concern work. She figured her mom was calling from her home in South

Carolina about the sonogram Minka sent her an hour ago.

"Hey, Mom."

"Hi, hon. How are you feeling?"

"Great, other than tired. Dr. Bailey gave us a good report today. According to their measurements, the baby's a couple of ounces bigger than usual, but she didn't estimate me to be farther along or anything. She told Caela I shouldn't deliver early, even if I'm rounder than Sadie. I guess I just have a chunk."

Her mom chuckled at the frank remark. *"Who doesn't love a chubby baby?"*

Minka agreed, caressing her belly. "I actually relented and let Wes and Caela learn the sex. They're merciless with their taunting."

"I heard. Wes texted Robin the news, but I refused to let him tell me. I'm sticking this out with my daughter."

"He did not! That traitor. Thank you for your loyalty. I appreciate having somebody on my side." She stuck her tongue out at her husband, who offered a devilish grin. After processing the development, she pondered her brother being in South Carolina instead of his apartment in Kissimmee. "I didn't know Robin was visiting you and Dad."

"That's my other reason for calling." Her serious tone made Minka straighten up on the lounge. *"Are you guilty of mail tampering if you pick up a package outside of a mailbox?"*

Minka relaxed a bit but not very much. "No, then you enter the realms of porch pirating, also known as third degree theft. What did he do?"

"Well, he and I are hunting down this jewel thief who's evading arrest, and—"

"Hold it right there! My brother roped you into scoring a bounty with him? Did he run out of gas money or what?"

"No, I wanted to help him, sweetie. This man needs to be stopped. He infiltrates jewelry stores by posing as a highly regarded appraiser—then robs them blind. He's made off with some two-million dollars' worth of merchandise. I just want to make sure we bring him down legally."

Minka let out a shout of laughter. "Mom, your son is a bounty hunter; hardly any of his methods are legal."

"Maybe that's true when he's alone, but when I'm here, I want the investigation to be above-ground. We located the suspect's father's house, and I persuaded Robin not to break-and-enter. But he wanted to look into a package by the guy's door to see if it contains any of the loot, and I told him I needed to check with you first."

He must love that, Minka thought with a smirk on her lips. "Is he there with you?"

"He went to the restroom, and I'm in the car. We parked at the gas station next door."

Minka debated how to answer the query before the slam of a car door interrupted her contemplation, and she heard Robin tell their mother it was nothing more than flavored water bought online.

"I told you to wait until we ran it by your sister," her mother insisted. *"She said this constitutes a third-degree crime."*

When he didn't respond, Minka was prompted to ask her mom, "He's drinking one of the bottles, isn't he?"

Robin released a delighted sigh. *"It's healthier than my soda. And I must remind you, sis, it's only considered a crime if I took more than three packages."*

Oddly enough, he had the troublesome fact correct, but his sister wouldn't let him off that easy. "But how many have you swiped in your honorable career?"

"None in South Carolina."

She couldn't suppress a momentary snicker. "Why are you enlisting our sixty-five-year-old mother in this operation?"

"Because she's watched so much news coverage on this dude, she has more insight into him than I do."

"She also has more scruples than you," Minka said.

"Yeah, that's the one snag," he admitted.

"Please, keep her safe. I'd like her here to welcome her new grandchild."

"Will do. Oh, and while we're on the subject, I'd like to suggest you continue your tradition of naming your kids after their uncles. Cael's had his day, so I should get mine. Besides, it can go for boy or girl, so it's a simple choice, seeing as you're too stubborn to find out."

"Mom let me pick out your name in the first place. I'm not sure I want to repeat that history."

"Why not? I turned out pretty awesome eventually."

She didn't argue the remark but offered that she and Wes would add it to their list. In case their escapades met with any peril, she trekked across the lawn so Caela could talk to them. The conversation proved humorous the instant Caela learned her grammy made the same decision as Minka about foregoing the gender reveal.

"But Grammy, you love to shop. You'll waste so much money by choosing the wrong kind of baby clothes."

The exchange concluded when the thief's father emerged from his garage and discovered his opened beverage pack. Minka hung up, anxious, but Wes admonished her to trust in her brother's expertise. After she mulled over the unsettling tip, she asked him, "How many people did you squeal to about our child's gender?"

He beamed. "The whole family and most of the precinct. Everyone's clued in on what you're carrying, except for you!"

"Me and my trustworthy mother."

"It's not my fault that they wanted to know," he teased.

Without a comeback, Minka tried to change the subject. "What's for dinner, anyhow?"

Her efforts proved to be a waste, as Wes gave her the speech she assumed he rehearsed. "*Gir*illed chicken with *boy*led peppers."

"And for dessert, *blue*berry ice cream with *pink* sprinkles!" Caela announced.

"Just what this baby needs today—more sugar," Minka joked.

The family's jovial moment together ended abruptly, with the ring of their neighbor's voice. "Well, hello there!"

Minka cringed, not a fan of the nosey woman. She wished she could duck behind the bushes like she usually did when she ventured into the backyard.

"Hi, Camille," Wes greeted.

"It seems like I haven't seen you in ages. I can see I haven't," she cried upon noticing Minka's pregnant belly. "I didn't realize you were expecting again!"

Minka grinned inside, proud she'd managed to keep the woman off her scent. It wasn't an accident, as she always entered the house through the garage and sent

Wes out for the mail since she began to show. She figured she couldn't escape her prying eyes for the entire nine months, but she celebrated making it this far.

"I wondered why you were adding onto the house. Looks like you should've started sooner to me."

"I'm not due until November," Minka told her, aware it was exactly what the woman—who they nicknamed 'Scoop' because of her gossipy nature—wanted to learn.

"Oh, no, you poor thing. As pregnant as can be all summer long, and it's already been a miserable one," she whined, hating the heat despite being a lifelong Florida resident. "I take it everything's going better than last time?"

Minka interpreted the question to be a reference to her history of miscarriages. "Yes, there haven't been any issues so far. Baby's heartbeat is strong, and we're both doing well."

Camille leveled a suspicious glance at Wes. "And Daddy's handling it well?"

Minka rolled her eyes, tired of Camille's assumption that Wes had run off because Minka was expecting Caela. In seven years, they couldn't convince her otherwise. To be fair, Minka had to admit the true story about his adventure in WITSEC didn't sound too believable.

Wes didn't try to argue but simply shrugged. "Of course. I could add on three more rooms if Minka's up for it."

"One at a time, babe," his wife stated, wishing he hadn't expressed his desire for more kids in front of Scoop. After all, she'd assumed Minka was pregnant six times since Caela's birth.

"And do we know if Caela's going to have a little brother or a little sister?" the woman pried.

Minka gave her husband a warning look, even signing the words *Traitor* and *Divorce* to him. While he understood the message loud and clear, their exuberant little girl wasn't as perceptive. "Well, Mommy doesn't—"

"We're going to be surprised this time," her father interrupted.

Caela murmured some words of protest, but thankfully, the older woman didn't pay any notice. "That's the way to go, if you ask me. Let God have that privilege. That's how I viewed it with my kids."

"It wasn't much of an option back then, was it?" Minka called her out with a coy grin, loving to get a subtle dig in here and there.

"I suppose not." Camille laughed it off but concluded her visit soon after.

Upon the neighbor's departure, Wes raised a brow at his satisfied wife, who shrugged. Despite the menu's theme, the baby banter subsided during dinner. With the evening breeze and storm earlier cooling down the high temperatures, they enjoyed their meal outside. Caela served the ice cream, which she layered with the pink sprinkles. Her mother couldn't figure if she was hinting at something or just loved to indulge in the sweets.

Regardless, she could only polish off half of the dessert. Besides it being too sweet, she feared neither she nor her unborn would sleep if she ate any more. She slid it over to Caela to finish and padded into the kitchen to wash the few dishes they used. As she loaded the dishwasher, her phone dinged with a text from Cael.

—We have another murder victim downtown. I'll

pick you up.—

****

One of the biggest differences Minka observed since switching to Homicide was her approach to a case. While she never took the seriousness of her career for granted, she could usually let her mind drift to her personal affairs on the drive to a crime scene. Now, on the other hand, her focus remained on the victim whose life had just been taken and the poor family who would be informed of their loss.

Still, she couldn't ignore Cael's smirk from behind the wheel. "They tipped you off, didn't they?"

"About what?"

Minka rolled her eyes. "Don't play dumb."

He chuckled. "You're not due for almost five more months. If Caela doesn't spill by then, Wes will."

"They couldn't keep it quiet for five minutes apparently."

Arriving at their destination, a parking lot of a closed mall, the two detectives put on their plastic gloves and climbed out of the car. Declan and his new partner, Henry Donahue, awaited them with Sadie. Her tired eyes told Minka that her fatigue was setting in, too, as she approached.

The unpleasant odor no longer sickened Minka, so she strode right up to the victim. "Who is he?"

Sadie seized the opening to tease her about the great gender debate. "I thought you told Wes not to let you know."

"I'm talking about the deceased man at our feet," Minka replied, wondering if her colleague truly revealed that she was having a son.

"Logan Baris," she reported. "Thirty-one years old,

16

from Wedgefield. He was shot twice in the chest; I'm guessing between five and six hours ago."

"When was it reported?" Minka asked.

"Around seven o'clock," Declan stated.

"Was there a phone on him?" Cael questioned.

Sadie shook her head. "Nope. His killer must've known better."

"Who called it in?" Cael inquired.

"A young passerby, who was going to the movies," Henry told them. "Ironically, she planned to see the latest horror flick, but she thinks she'll opt for the rom-com, instead."

Tickled by her newest colleague's resilient sense of humor, she shook her head before deciding how to proceed. "With the mall closed and apparently no other witnesses, Cael and I will try to contact his next-of-kin. Tomorrow, we can find out if we can get our hands on surveillance."

With that, the five parted ways for the night, Minka and Cael retreating to her house for their impromptu investigation. Their research took longer than usual, with it difficult to locate any of Baris's relatives. His parents had both passed away, and his only brother, Luca, worked on a cruise ship, like he did. Unfortunately, Luca was at sea and wouldn't be back for two more days, according to his voicemail greeting. Though the detectives preferred to talk to loved ones in person, they left a message for him, asking him to call them at his earliest convenience.

Surprising them, he made the international call from a dock in Antigua while they were at the precinct the next morning. When Cael greeted the victim's brother, Luca uncomfortably cleared his throat, a common gesture among those who were contacted by police. Minka allowed Cael to take control of the devastating conversation, as he usually did. It was the worst part of the job for both of them but especially emotional to her, given her already hormonal state. Thus, her brother-in-law agreed to shoulder the brunt of the condolence speeches, at least until after her maternity leave.

The exchange proceeded just like many others, with a distraught Luca pleading for answers. They couldn't give him many, but they had to ask some of him.

"How long has it been since you saw Logan?" Minka questioned.

"Just over three months." He choked out the words, but he mustered up more strength to continue. *"February's slow for both of us, so we always arrange to meet up then."*

Cael tried to fill in the gaps they still had in his background. "What's the name of the ship he works on?"

"The Exquisite Marvel."

"What were his duties?" Minka asked.

"He was a waiter by day, but at night, he performed in the cabaret shows. Singing was his passion. He was even close to signing a recording contract a few years ago. When it fell through, he took the job on the ship, but he still wanted more."

"Was he continuing to pursue a career to your knowledge?" Minka replied.

"He mentioned several travelers who were in the business and approached him after listening to him, but I'm not sure it ever went further than that."

"Why did the recording contract go south on him?" Cael inquired.

"The studio, Seeley Entertainment, didn't want him

to make the music he wanted to. One of their head honchos discovered him at a gig and liked what he heard, but when they stuck him in the sound booth, they wanted him to completely change his style. They said they wouldn't release anything else. It was ugly."

"Ugly enough to lead to this?" Minka asked.

"Given how long it's been since then, I wouldn't think so, but he hardly visited Orlando for any other reason."

After doing some quick research, Cael muted the phone and showed his findings to Minka. "The studio's only a few blocks from where the body was dumped."

****

Arriving at the studio for Seeley Entertainment, Minka regarded the plain building, which didn't compare to the glamorous settings Nashville or Los Angeles probably offered. In a small shopping outlet, the location was somewhat hidden away. Still, Minka supposed many hopefuls had driven up to it in eager expectation, anxious to get their dreams off the ground.

She and Cael made their way inside, escaping the summer heat, and approached the receptionist. "May we speak with Mr. Losche?" Minka requested, opting not to show her badge so as not to cause a stir.

Taken aback, the woman paused before advising them in a whisper, "With no disrespect, I don't think you two are what we're looking for here."

Minka crossed her arms. "I think a pregnant deaf woman and her reasonably good-looking brother-in-law could have a singing career, but that isn't why we came."

Cael revealed his badge. "We have a few questions about a former client."

"I see," she replied, her tone reserved. "Well, he's

busy with an artist at the moment, but he should be finished shortly. Can I ask you to wait?"

"Sure. We'll use the time to rehearse," Minka told her.

Cael shook his head at her once they were seated, and proud of herself, she signed, *Dream crusher!* Unable to stifle a snicker, he glanced away, until the woman allowed them to meet with the studio's manager. Despite the suite's low-key appearance, they found Seeley Losche's office to be expensively furnished and adorned with accolades—albeit for songs and vocalists that Minka didn't recognize.

After exchanging formal introductions, Cael cut to the chase. "We're investigating the death of a singer you worked with some time ago, Logan Baris. I'm assuming you remember him?"

"Vaguely," he acknowledged, but his expression showed it to be an understatement. "So many kids pass through our doors, and it's difficult to put a face to every name. I was fairly familiar with Logan. Nice guy. I'm sorry to learn of his passing, especially at his young age."

"I'd say you'd have to be fairly familiar with him, having offered him a recording contract and all," Minka said.

"It's actually more common than you might think, Detective."

"Word is, though, your business together was short-lived," Cael continued. "His brother told us you two had some differences, and the deal fell through."

"It did, unfortunately. Logan was very talented, but as I recall, he was inclined to hold himself back. I tried to push him to his full potential, but he resisted my prodding."

"Did that struggle ever become heated?" Minka inquired.

Losche leaned back in his pleather chair. "There were some passionate words exchanged, but it didn't go any further than that. We parted on decent terms."

"Have you contacted him since?" Cael questioned.

"No," he denied in a brisk manner. "That's about all I have to share with you guys, so unless I can help you with anything else, I have to get back to my clients."

Minka and Cael gave each other a thoughtful glance, silently debating whether or not to ask Losche for his alibi. With no evidence against him, they decided against it and departed the studio empty-handed. Upon returning to the precinct, they ascertained that Declan and Henry had a more successful morning, having scoped through surveillance to determine that Baris's body had been thrown from a blue SUV. Tracing the license plate revealed it to be recently reported stolen from a car garage at the same dock where the ship he worked on picked up its passengers.

"So it was taken while the none-the-wiser owners were having caviar and island hopping," Minka stated.

"Have you called the local PD?" Cael asked.

"Yes, but they haven't made much progress," Declan said. "Surveillance only showed two hooded guys hotwiring it and taking off Wednesday morning."

"Any insight into the owners?" Cael asked them.

"Not much more than Minka assumed," Henry admitted. "Middle-aged couple, off on a ten-day excursion."

Pondering it further, Minka theorized aloud, "Could Logan have been one of the thieves?"

"We can't rule it out," Henry stated, "as it happened

before his estimated time of death. Plus, *The Exquisite Marvel* had just docked earlier."

With everything pointing back to the cruise ship, they sought to make contact with the crew. They wondered if it'd be possible, given it set sea that evening and wouldn't return until Monday. They tracked down the ship's information and placed a call to the control room, but nobody answered at the time.

Not long afterward, they called Logan Baris's landlord and were granted access to his Wedgefield apartment. They spotted Logan's beige pickup truck in the parking lot with a parking pass from the cruise port garage hanging off his rear-view mirror. If he had the habit of leaving it during the ship's voyages, they concluded he wouldn't have reason to join the car thieves in their escapades. Upon going inside, the landlord led them up to the victim's fourth-floor apartment. Minka was nearly out of breath after the long climb—which didn't begin to prepare her for what awaited them inside the residence.

Surveying the blood-splattered room, she deduced the obvious. "I'd say we've found the scene of the crime."

Chapter Two

After forensics collected samples and dusted the room for prints, Cael and Minka asked the landlord for recordings from surveillance cameras from the past forty-eight hours. On the drive to the precinct, Minka focused on Logan Baris's phone, which they'd recovered from a corner in the front room. No doubt lost during the scuffle, it was of primary concern, and despite having to view it through plastic, they hoped it would unlock vital insight into the man's final hours.

Minka rattled off the names of the contacts he'd last texted. As she did so, they all sounded familiar, but for the life of her, she couldn't place any of them.

Cael explained why. "Given those are all alter egos of superheroes, the man kept some powerful company."

"Guess he didn't want anyone knowing his friends."

"What were they discussing?"

She tapped on the top conversation from yesterday, which began with a decisive proclamation from Logan.

—*I can't do this anymore. It's wrong. Last time was too close of a call, and I want out.*—

The recipient, BW, replied in a passive-aggressive tone.

—*That's your choice, but if you squeal, your profits will suddenly be useless to you.*—

"I guess the profits are useless in death," Cael replied after Minka read the back-and-forth to him. "Our next move should be checking his financials."

Once at their desks, he ran Baris's information through the database, while Minka continued to contemplate the exchange. "Profits from what?"

"Maybe masquerading as comic book vigilantes?"

"But why would they be worried Logan would expose them?"

Cael's eyes widened. "Because they're actually the real deal."

She gave him a teasing shove. "You are too much like your brother."

The results of the financial search appeared on the screen, sending them both back to reality. "If his earnings were really worth threatening," Cael muttered, "they aren't in his bank account. In fact, the only deposits are his regular wages from the cruise line."

"I suppose that makes sense. Nobody would have an easy time taking money from his personal account. If it's an illegal scheme, he'd probably be paid in cash or a separate account."

Cael quickly moved on from the apparent dead end. "Let's run those phone numbers and unmask these wannabes."

Holding her breath, Minka observed his fingers at work. All too soon, the effort seemed to be in vain. "Unregistered. It figures."

Both of them leaned back in their chairs, defeated, as Minka searched the phone further for any more clues it had to yield. Before long, however, her own phone rang. Recognizing Sadie's ID, she put it on speaker for Cael's benefit. "What's going on, girl?"

"I just ran the blood samples CSU dropped off from Baris's apartment," she said. *"Believe it or not, it isn't*

Logan's blood type."

Cael sighed. "So, we have one body in a double homicide."

"And that isn't my only reason for calling," the medical examiner replied, her voice hesitant. *"I've never had to say this, but it appears Logan Baris's gunshot wounds are post-mortem. Something else killed him."*

"And his killer wanted it to appear he was fatally shot," Minka said.

"It would seem that way."

"But why?" Cael wondered aloud. "It isn't like shooting him is going to make his death inconspicuous."

"Have you found anything else that could've caused his death?" Minka asked.

"I'm seeing some narrowing of the airways in his lung, but that could be caused by asthma. The nicotine residue on his fingers tells me he was a smoker, so the restriction comes as no surprise. At any rate, I'm running some blood work now, and I just finished the toxicology screening. Of course, I won't have those results for weeks."

Unable to wait around for technology to do the investigating for them, they had to stick to tried and true methods. Now, with two victims on their hands, they accessed the surveillance footage Logan's landlord gave them from the hallway right in front of Baris's door. They searched through events of the past two days. They cued the footage up to Wednesday and soon discovered Logan Baris had arrived home, alone, just before noon. He remained inside for two hours—until two hooded guys showed up at his door. Once he answered, they plowed in, using force. After busting past him, the door remained shut for several minutes, during which Minka and Cael only guessed what was happening. Regardless, the three reemerged and exited the building together. As they rounded the corner, a separate camera captured Logan being prodded with a gun to his back.

"What time did he send that text about wanting out?" Cael asked Minka.

She consulted the log she'd made of his phone calls. "One-thirty."

"Twenty minutes before these clowns showed up at his door."

"Maybe the guy didn't take his resignation as well as he let on," Minka replied.

They continued to pour through the surveillance footage, looking to determine if Logan and his captors ever resurfaced. They didn't spot him again but observed another man coming and going into the apartment frequently throughout the day, twice in workout gear and once on an apparent grocery run. They presumed him to be Logan's roommate. A few minutes to midnight, the day took a turn for the worse, when the same two hooded men appeared again, banging on the door to coerce the guy to let them inside.

"Didn't Declan and Henry say there were two hooded guys who stole that SUV?" Minka asked. When her partner nodded, she continued, "These two could've been the same ones."

"It's possible. Then again, wearing hoods while engaging in criminal activity is hardly original."

"Maybe we could get in touch with the department there and compare the footage."

He agreed with her suggestion, but first, they both stared at the screen to discern where this second visit led. After Cael sped twenty-five minutes ahead, the door reopened and the figures emerged. This time, the two hooded individuals were captured assisting a man, bloodied and barely walking, out of the building.

Minka gasped in astonishment, unable to believe he'd survived the amount of blood loss they'd seen at the apartment. "He's alive."

"At least he was thirty-six hours ago."

****

Minka and Cael called Logan's landlord, who informed them that Logan shared the apartment with a man named Emmett Bouscay. They then retrieved his personal information from the database and concluded he matched the description of the man dragged out of the apartment building. Twenty-nine years old, Bouscay had shared the apartment with Logan for the past seven months. Before that, he'd lived on one of the upper floors in the building since graduating from college. He had one DUI arrest on his record, but that dated back to his fraternity days. He'd stayed on the straight and narrow after that, leaving little on his recent past. Resorting to a quest into social media, they found his last post from Tuesday evening to be a simple picture of the night sky.

While Cael continued to research Bouscay, Minka scanned through Logan's phone for any recent correspondence between the two. Right when she surmised it held nothing of interest, she discovered an unsent draft to Emmett.

—*It's over. Thanks, man.*—

She showed her partner the message. "Look at this. It was saved ten minutes after he told the superheroes he wanted out. I'd say he didn't live up to his agreement not to reveal the heroes' exploits."

"It appears so, but we can't get ahead of ourselves.

He could've been relieved about anything being over."

After putting out an APB to other departments in the area and a missing person's report, they contacted Emmett's family. His parents were divorced, and both lived out of state, so his sister proved to be their best resource. With her a stay-at-home mom in the suburbs, they made the short trip to have a face-to-face conversation with Iris Wickers.

The woman opened the door right away. "Is this about my brother?"

"Yes, Mrs. Wickers, it is," Minka replied after she showed her ID.

Iris invited them inside and explained her abruptness. "My mom just called and told me. I'm sorry if I seem on-edge."

"It's understandable," Cael replied with compassion. "You and Emmett are close?"

"Closer than anyone else in our family, but that isn't saying a lot. We speak pretty often, and he's great with my kids."

"When did you last hear from him?" Minka inquired.

"Just Wednesday morning. We didn't talk for long, but nothing seemed unusual. We were planning a camping trip later this month, and he was firming up the details with me. I guess I'll have to cancel our reservations."

Her emotional statement touched Minka. "Hopefully, you won't."

Seeming grateful for the reassurance, Iris offered for them to sit. Cael took a seat on the sunroom's couch beside his partner before continuing, "Do you know of anyone who had something against your brother?"

"Not really. Then again, he's never been one to open up much, not even as a kid, so I can't be sure he would've told me if there were somebody."

Following through on the strategy they'd formulated on the way, Minka took her turn. "Emmett's roommate, Logan, was killed the same day he went missing. Did he ever mention him to you?"

"Occasionally," she answered in a hesitant tone. "The two of them seemed to get along well, but Emmett also enjoyed having the apartment to himself for the most part."

"So, did he shoulder the brunt of the expenses?" Cael inquired.

"No, they split them fifty-fifty, which really helped Emmett. They were both struggling with the rent, and they started chatting about it in the laundry room. Logan said he was just gone too much to carry it all, so they struck a deal."

Minka sensed there was still more that Iris was reluctant to share, so she dug deeper. "Did you ever meet Logan?"

"I didn't." Iris lowered her head. "Emmett said he didn't want the kids around him."

"Did he tell you why?" Cael questioned.

She shook her head. "I asked him once, but he didn't give me a true explanation. After that, I didn't press him. He loves them, and I figured if he considered it to be in their best interest not to be in Logan's company, that's all I needed to hear. I should've known it was just as dangerous for Emmett to be living with him. Please, tell me you don't think he'll be killed, too."

Unable to give her a direct answer, Minka crossed the room and leaned toward her. "My little brother was taken once, too. Thankfully, he was returned safely to us and is still around to annoy me to this day. We're going to do our utmost to get the same outcome for you."

Her wry comment evoked a grin to Iris's face, and they took their leave on a slightly bright note. Meanwhile, the rest of Minka and Cael's day wasn't too productive. Sadie had nothing new on Logan's true cause of death, nor despite repeated attempts were they able to contact anyone from the cruise ship. They continued to peer through traffic cameras stationed throughout downtown Orlando for even a glimpse of the blue SUV that had been used to dump Baris's body. To their frustration, they were unable to spot even a trace of it.

As they started to pack up for the night, their captain, Gus Channing, entered the station, having just returned from a conference in Washington, DC.

"Welcome back," Minka greeted him.

"Thanks, and congratulations! Wes texted me the news."

She smirked, aware of where this would lead. "Yes, we are having a human. You can never be sure these days."

Her comeback subdued him for a brief moment. "I'm not a big one on souvenirs, but this screamed your husband's name."

Taking the bag he handed her, she extracted the phony 'FBI' cap. "Why do you hate me? I'm trying to keep him out of WITSEC for this pregnancy."

"It's a gag gift, Minks. I'm pretty sure he's outgrown his days of playing law-enforcer."

"Yeah, until you dress him up to look like a professional!"

The guys snickered at her comment, before Gus

made one last joke. "I bought something for the baby, too, but I guess I picked the wrong color."

****

The day's disturbing revelations had sapped Minka of energy. She staggered into the kitchen where Wes was reheating yesterday's leftovers for the family's dinner. His wife made a bee-line to the sparkling grape juice she'd bought to celebrate their wedding anniversary last month. She took a long swig, straight from the bottle.

"Wild woman!"

"In my mind, it's vodka."

He snickered and cupped her bump with his palm. "How's our little one doing?"

"Probably better than me."

"After that drink of yours, I'm not so sure."

To prove her point, she elaborated, "Our gunshot victim was killed by something other than a gun; he's probably a criminal, and his roommate was beaten half-dead then abducted last night. So, yes, I'd say our twenty-one-week-old fetus had a better day, floating along the lazy river of Casa Del Minka."

Wes laughed and took her in his arms, kissing her neck. "That's my favorite resort."

She giggled and reciprocated his advances, drawing him closer.

Not a second later, Caela cried, "Mrs. Paletta's here!"

The two parted, the moment over. They debated over which one of them would handle Camille, until both managed to drag each other to the door. Once Minka spotted that their neighbor wasn't alone, she realized the usual amount of groaning her visits incited wouldn't suffice this time.

"There are the parents-to-be," Camille sang.

"Is she pregnant?" squawked the green parrot from the cage Mrs. Paleta used to transport the bird.

Caela skipped over for a closer look. "Wow! That bird's really smart!"

The older woman blushed for the first time since Minka and Wes met her. "I apologize, Minka. I'm afraid Fritzi has picked up some expressions I didn't intend her to. She loves to eavesdrop."

Like owner, like pet. "It's fine. At least she's right in this case."

She couldn't tell if Scoop registered the subtle jab to her own faulty intuition, but she quickly moved on. "I meant to ask you this the other day, but your wonderful news made me forget all about it. Victor and I are going to visit our grandkids in Kansas, and we need someone to take care of Fritzi. We usually drive and take her with us, but with Vic's bad back and my lame hip, we decided to fly."

Caela clasped her hands together. "Can we keep her, Mom? Please?"

Uneager to have a miniature Camille in the house, Minka stalled. "How long will you be away?"

"Six days."

"I mean, we're gone so much, and when we are here, Caela's noisy, and Wes is hammering up in the new baby's room, and..."

"I'll be quiet, Mommy. I promise," her daughter pleaded. "And Daddy needs a break."

Wes tried to intervene. "Maybe we'll talk it over. When are you guys leaving?"

"In five minutes."

****

32

Fritzi's first night at the Avery house ensued with the ruckus Minka predicted. After Camille took off, the parrot chirped and squealed nonstop, especially once she observed her owners depart their driveway from the window. After that, Caela tried to comfort the bird, thus adding to the volume. Minka remedied the problem by simply taking her cochlear out, provoking a wrathful scowl from her husband.

"You're the one who agreed to this," she reminded him.

The words resonated all night, with Fritzi forgoing sleep to continue her tirade. Deaf to it all, Minka awoke well-rested Saturday morning, while Wes could barely open his swollen eyes. Ever the early riser, Caela wandered downstairs before either of them and sat right in front of the birdcage.

"Did you sleep through that ruckus, sweetie?" Wes questioned the little one.

"Not really, but I didn't mind. It'll be the same way when the baby comes."

"She has a point, Daddy," Minka teased, trotting down the stairs behind him.

"Is she pregnant?" Fritzi cried again.

Caela wasn't impressed by the pet's intuition this time around. "I don't think she understands you actually are, Mom. She asked me the same thing when I came down."

Minka commended her insight, though she silently fumed when she imagined the various occasions the bird would've heard the phrase...just when it concerned her. She couldn't fathom how many other women were victims to Camille's insatiable scrutiny.

Still, she shook it off, going on to begin her day as

usual. She checked her phone for any overnight developments on the Emmett Bouscay case. Finding none, she waited for Sadie, who was riding with her to their first Lamaze class.

She hadn't planned to take a birthing course again, but wanting a companion, Sadie convinced her she needed a refresher. Minka could've waited a bit longer to register, but as she neared her sixth month, Sadie was eager to start the eight-week program. Minka didn't mind, aware she'd process the information better before she entered her third trimester.

When Sadie padded up the sidewalk, Minka grinned, awaiting the exchange between her and Fritzi.

The crazy bird didn't disappoint. "Is she pregnant?"

Sadie's mouth dropped open. "Finally, someone who believes me without seeing the sonogram!"

Minka laughed. "It's pretty apparent now. Don't you think she's catching up with me, Caela?"

The girl wandered over and gave a gentle squeeze to both bumps, her expression contemplative. "I'd still say you have a few more popped kernels, Mom."

Her mother ruffled her brown hair, while Sadie stared in confusion. Minka told her friend, "I'll explain later. You didn't get any updates from CSU, did you?"

She shook her head. "Their tests take as long as mine, if not longer. I'm still reeling from everything that happened yesterday."

"Me, too."

The ladies halted the shop talk and headed over to their class. For the initial session, they opted to leave their husbands at home, with the program's outline saying partners wouldn't be involved until the third week. From past experience, Minka learned letting Wes accompany her only led to embarrassment.

This morning's class followed the scheduled agenda, as the instructor discussed early labor signs and the benefits of a natural birth. A lot of fraternizing ensued afterward around the fruit salad one of the women made. Living up to her predictions, all of the other students were first-time moms. The majority knew the gender of their babies, with Sadie and nine others expecting girls and five awaiting boys.

One of them told Sadie, "I don't know how anybody can wait to find out."

Sadie slid a precarious glance at Minka. "It's exciting either way."

"Maybe, but I can't figure how you can bond with your baby without a clue who's in there."

Minka ventured away, not caring to defend her choice to a lady with such strong opinions. Still, the words pierced her.

Sadie addressed the uncomfortable moment on the drive home. "I'm sorry if Phoebe offended you."

"Thank you. I understand her sentiment. I viewed things differently during my first pregnancy, too. This time, my priorities have shifted altogether. A year ago, I didn't expect to get to do this again because of our fertility issues. Now that this baby is growing inside me, I just want to savor every second without obsessing over the future."

Sadie squeezed her hand and conveyed how happy she was for her. She hesitated before indulging her curiosity. "You don't have to answer this if you don't want to, but did you guys seek help?"

"No, we couldn't afford the major treatments. Plus, we both agreed Caela enriched our lives so much on her own and that we'd be content if we remained a family of three. We stopped stressing and recalibrated everything back to our love, and here we are. It didn't hurt to get away from our intrusive neighbor for a weekend, either. For a woman who always wants a baby in me, she sure is effective birth control!"

They both laughed, with Minka having told her about Camille's inopportune timing yesterday.

Minka switched on her turn signal as they approached her street. "But Caela still insists your pregnancy rubbed off on me."

Her friend giggled. "You're welcome."

Sadie expressed the various ways the prospect of motherhood altered her view of matters and how her protective instinct surprised her. Her sentiments reminded Minka of Emmett's shielding his family from Logan. Deep down, she still believed his reluctance reaffirmed the fact that Logan was involved in some shady activity.

Then again, she supposed, there could be plenty of innocent reasons why Emmett didn't want his family around his roommate. For instance, maybe Logan wasn't good with kids, and he thought it'd make for an uncomfortable visit. On the other hand, what if it had less to do with Logan's secrets and more to do with something Logan could divulge about his friend? Many brothers withheld subjects from their sisters, including her own.

Upon arriving at the house, Sadie hopped right into her crossover and took off to meet her husband for lunch. Minka retreated inside, tuned out Fritzi, and started preparing her family's meal. The commotion upstairs told her Wes and Sal, Gus's handyman father-in-law, were busy in the new room, so she wanted to fix them something hearty to contribute to the job.

While she toasted some bread for paninis, she tidied up the kitchen, one chore Wes overlooked when he was in charge. Little by little, they granted Caela access to the candy drawer, but she, too, needed some tips on being neat. A couple of bags lay cluttered on the granite counter, and Minka started to tuck them away until she noted one had only a single snack-bar left. Just then, Cael entered the room.

"Hey," she greeted him. "Would you like a candy bar? I just noticed it's the last one."

"Nah, I think I'd better cut back. That bird in there just asked if I'm pregnant."

"Wes and I've been wondering that, too!"

"Ha ha," he replied with sarcasm, crossing his arms. "It isn't easy keeping the pounds off when your partner has a loaded snack drawer she's constantly opening."

"It's called motherhood," Minka retorted as she defiantly crunched into the candy bar. "Jokes aside, I've been thinking over our interview with Iris Wickers yesterday and how she said Emmett didn't want her children in Logan's company. Of course, it initially disturbed me, but I'm starting to question if we're overestimating his reason behind it. Just because his roommate wants to keep his family separate from him doesn't mean he's an outlaw."

"That's true. Logan could have a judgmental bird that might insult them. Then again, we can't forget those texts you found about him wanting out of something. I can pass off one as possibly being more minor than it seems, but both tidbits combined make it quite suspicious."

She couldn't help but agree with him, with all the signals pointing to their victim being caught up in an unscrupulous scheme of some kind. In her new position, she sometimes found it difficult to accept a victim's own guilt in his demise, especially after she witnessed his helpless body laying cold. All too often, though, she had to face it head-on, and this appeared to be one of those occasions. Still, she strived to keep an open mind.

"Did you make any headway this morning?" Minka asked her partner.

"No, but I wanted to drop by so we both could make another attempt to contact *The Exquisite Marvel* crew. According to the itinerary of their current voyage, this is their day at sea, with no ports-of-call. Maybe we'll have better success."

True to Cael's logic, a man's voice answered, renewing Minka's optimism.

"I'm calling in regard to one of your staff members, Logan Baris," Cael explained after introducing himself.

Being one of the ship captain's assistants in the cockpit, the man wasn't familiar with the name and put them on hold to retrieve the cruise director. Once on the line, Spencer Franklin told them, *"Logan isn't on the ship right now. He's attending to a family emergency."*

Having spoken to his only surviving family member—the brother—who'd made no mention of such emergency, the detectives exchanged a cynical glance. Nonetheless, Cael didn't express their skepticism. "I'm afraid it's turned into a personal one. He was discovered dead two days ago."

"Oh, my. I'm sorry to hear that. Logan was a good worker."

"When did he ask for some time off?" Minka asked.

"*Tuesday. We were docked, and he tracked me down to request a leave of absence once we returned to Port Canaveral.*"

"Did he indicate how long he expected to be gone?" Cael inquired.

"*He hoped for only one voyage, but he wasn't certain. I was actually going to give him a call this afternoon to see if he planned to be aboard for our next one.*"

"And this wasn't common for him, to take an unplanned leave?" Cael questioned.

"*No. He took a vacation once a year or so, but he hasn't missed a day, otherwise.*"

Minka recalled that two were involved in the car theft and Emmett's abduction. "Did any other crew members depart the ship at the same time as Logan?"

"*No, everyone else has been here,*" Franklin reported.

"Is he particularly close to anyone who might be able to tell us more about his recent behavior?" Minka tried.

"*Not to my knowledge. Sure, the ones he worked with most probably knew him better than I did, but he didn't pal around a lot on a social basis. I suppose that's what made him such a useful employee.*"

They requested he give their information to those coworkers in case they had insight into anything useful and thanked him for his time.

Sighing over the lackluster conversation, Minka offered to make her partner a sandwich. He declined, needing to get home to Autumn, his wife, and their two-year-old son, Tyson. Right before he departed, a phone call delayed him. The exchange didn't last long, and

Minka observed his urgency grow as it wrapped up.

"Our stolen SUV was just spotted at a rest stop on the turnpike," he declared.

Chapter Three

Minka and Cael pulled up to the scene and found a waiting ambulance, idling at the scene, while paramedics attended to a bloody and weak Emmett Bouscay. The blue SUV from multiple tapes was parked to the side, abandoned.

"We're relieved to see you alive, Mr. Bouscay," Minka greeted him.

Emmett nodded and managed to lift a meager thumbs-up.

"Do you know who abducted you?" Cael questioned.

He weakly shook his head, prompting the paramedics to stop the interview because of their patient's condition. The detectives understood but were still discouraged that they couldn't get answers to their many unresolved questions. They observed the EMTs wheel the gurney with their patient to the ambulance and drive away, lights flashing but with sirens silent.

The detecting work wasn't finished, however, as they rushed inside to discern if anybody had witnessed the kidnappers escape. Since so many drivers passed by the rest area—and at a rapid pace—it was unlikely anyone who had been were there long enough to be privy to the actual moment. The SUV was already abandoned by the time the state trooper who reported its discovery had entered the parking lot. Thus, their only recourse—

and perhaps the best one—was to consult surveillance tapes provided by Florida Department of Transportation.

Employing the assistance of the security guards, Minka and Cael backed up the footage and found that the SUV appeared an hour earlier. Neither driver nor the front seat passenger, both still in hoods, emerged until a white van picked them up and raced back onto the turnpike. All the while, the plates and make of the van were hidden from the camera's view.

CSU worked on collecting prints from the SUV but soon reported there weren't any visible ones to be had, apart from the bloody spot where Bouscay must've sat. The steering wheel appeared to have been wiped clean, as did all of the other surfaces. Nonetheless, they gave it a thorough examination, snapping pictures and swabbing the carpet for fluids or residue.

After the techs concluded their duties, Minka and Cael could inspect it for themselves. Given that it wasn't the criminals' personal vehicle, it resembled a rental after it was returned, with no belongings left behind. Unfortunately for the actual owners, the thieves didn't leave the keys behind, either. What they couldn't take with them, however, held the most value of all—the navigation system.

There hadn't been any recent GPS searches entered, but using some of the techy skills she acquired over her career, Minka accessed the log of their locations. After departing Logan Baris's apartment the second time, the outlaws went to Lake Poinsett, an hour's drive south of Orlando, before their latest trek up the turnpike. Taking down the coordinates, Cael and Minka set back out on the road.

Consulting their own GPS, they were led to what

looked to be the site of a derelict lake house. The property was overgrown with weeds but did reveal a set of tracks where the SUV had no doubt been parked—in front of an old shed, the perfect setting to hold someone captive.

Stepping out of the car, Minka commented, "A pregnant, deaf woman going into a secluded shed— sounds like the start of a horror movie."

"I'll protect you," her partner teased.

The wood door stood ajar when they approached it, and both detectives held a cautionary hand on their holsters as Cael opened it the rest of the way. Without a working light, they used the one on each of their phones to illuminate the area. Circling through it, they discovered a chair in the middle with untied ropes around it and a bloody hammer beside it.

Cael sighed. "Looks like we'd better call out forensics again."

****

CSU arrived within an hour, only to draw the same conclusion they had about the SUV, with no traces of fingerprints on the surfaces. Still being as meticulous as possible, they completed their work. After that, Minka and Cael checked out several local establishments to ask if anyone noticed the SUV or suspicious activity. They struck out at the restaurant, gas station, and store nearby, making one last stop at a café. Nobody helped them there, either, but they opted to use the opportunity to get a mid-afternoon snack before heading back to Orlando.

While waiting for their food in the slowest-moving line ever recorded, Cael scanned the newspaper, with Minka glancing over it from beside him. A headline about the area's rise in heroin overdoses caught her attention, conjuring a new angle of the case, but she chose not to voice it in such a public setting.

Once they settled into Cael's car, however, she took a sip of her decaf iced coffee and began speculating. "Do you think Logan could've been involved in the trafficking of drugs or something else? Being on a ship all year and stopping at these poor islands would make it convenient."

"Drug lords don't care about convenience. Plus, I'm sure the cruise's security measures would prevent that."

"Unless there were others on the inside. After all, the SUV was stolen from the port the same afternoon Logan took off for home. What if they were coworkers who followed him?"

"Wouldn't they keep their vehicles at the port, too, though? Why steal one you don't need?"

She followed his reasoning and accepted it but still kept the possibility in her mind. "Do you really believe he left the ship on account of an emergency?"

"Probably one of some sort. He clearly wanted to get out of whatever he and the superheroes were up to. That's another sign that his exploits were on the mainland."

"But the SUV was taken from the port and used to dump his body hours later," she reminded him. "It simply doesn't add up that the thieves—and most likely, Logan's murderers—weren't there with him."

Cael paused for a moment, before he nodded his head. "I think we'd better get over to *The Exquisite Marvel* when it docks on Monday."

Minka agreed with her partner, pleased she persuaded him to her logic. She exhaled, enjoying the first lull in her busy day. Despite her reservations, she checked her phone and discovered a slew of messages from her mom. Initially, she tensed, afraid the bounty hunt had gone awry, but she laughed once she read through them all. "I'm sure my mother is driving Robin bonkers. She keeps asking if his various tactics are lawful. Her last one was about him hacking into someone else's Wi-Fi."

He chuckled. "And I'll bet he insists that we all do that because he's seen it on television."

She murmured a word of acknowledgement and called her mom. When she didn't answer, Minka tried her brother's phone, switching on her speaker for Cael's sake in anticipation of an entertaining exchange.

Robin muttered a distracted greeting. "*Huh?*"

"Good afternoon to you, too." She grinned at Cael. "Is Mom there with you? I just called her, but she didn't pick up."

"*Nah, she decided to go home to Dad. I think she figured it would be more exciting than all of the stakeouts and investigative research. You understand.*"

"I sure do." His sister suppressed a snort. She noted the clicking of keystrokes in the background and gathered that he was indeed busy hacking. "Any leads on your crook?"

"*No, his father has really sturdy fire-walls—I mean window curtains. I can't get a peek inside.*" The tapping continued until he let out a groan. A slam followed, no doubt him closing his laptop. She almost concluded the conversation, but he changed the subject. "*By the way, have you and Wes talked about my suggestion the other day?*"

The question puzzled her at first, but the movement in her womb made her catch on. "No, we haven't had much time to discuss the baby's name any further. But I must remind you that we named Caela after Cael because he almost took a bullet for me when I was pregnant. So you'd better think up a valiant act to win us over."

Silence filled the line for a beat, with Minka winking over at Cael. Finally, her brother offered a proposition. *"Would you like to go paintballing with me?"*

****

By the time Minka arrived home, Wes and Sal had finished working on the nursery for the day, with her husband sweeping up the sawdust they'd trekked into the house. She made up a quick skillet meal from the freezer, without time to thaw out anything else for dinner. Once they all sat down, Minka endeavored to dismiss the case for the evening and enjoy the time with her family.

Though her due date still lay months away, she could already sense their time as a trio drawing to a close. Caela welcomed the expansion to their family from the instant she figured out her mom was expecting, but Minka understood the life-altering change that awaited all of them. Caela had been an only child for seven years, much longer than the three Minka had before Robin's birth. They'd developed their routine over that time period, with the little girl soaking up her parents' exclusive attention. The new baby would soon put a ripple in that pattern, so Wes and Minka made every effort to show her undivided devotion while they could.

Thankfully, their night proved to be relaxing and uninterrupted, except for a couple of outbursts from Fritzi. After her mom returned her call and reminded her of their custom with the cockatiel Minka had as a kid, she covered the bird's cage with a blanket before they retreated to bed. The tip afforded them a peaceful slumber.

For the second day straight, Minka and Cael couldn't take the weekend easy, with the hospital informing Cael that Emmett Bouscay was now in stable condition and agreed to speak with them. It hadn't even been twenty-four hours since he'd been freed, but Emmett seemed better. With the swelling in his face decreased, and his bruises far less noticeable, he gave them a friendly smile upon their entry into the room. They commented on his recovery and expressed their relief that he was safe.

"Same here, detectives," Emmett agreed. "I appreciate what you did to find me and don't think I'd be alive if you hadn't. Once they learned of the alert you'd posted about me, they figured I was more of a liability to them than anything."

Minka began the questioning. "Did you recognize your captors?"

"No. They wore hoods or masks the whole time, so I don't even know what they looked like. All I can say is they're friends of my roommate Logan. They kept mentioning him in a familiar way."

"Is that why they did this to you?" Cael inquired.

Emmett nodded. "They thought I had insight into a business deal they made. They tortured me until I convinced them that I didn't."

"Was that the truth?" Minka asked.

"For the most part," he acknowledged. "All Logan ever told me was that he was involved in something he never should've touched."

"Were they coworkers of his or just acquaintances?" Cael inquired.

"I wish I could tell you."

"How many were there?" Minka questioned.

"Two, I think," he replied, reminding her again of the car thieves.

"I don't suppose they mentioned where they were headed yesterday?" Minka inquired.

He shook his head.

"Did they tell you Logan's dead?" she continued.

"I gathered that. They kept threatening me that I'd end up like him if I didn't cooperate."

"When did you last see Logan?" Cael asked.

"He came home briefly a few weeks ago for a change of wardrobe, but I haven't seen him since."

"How did he act when you saw him?" Minka asked.

"He was unhappier than usual, I'd say. Mind you, he wasn't normally Mr. Sunshine, so I didn't think too much of it."

She deemed this the ideal opportunity to unearth more of his feelings toward Logan. "When we spoke to your sister, she indicated that you had reservations about your family meeting Logan. Could you tell us why?"

Emmett shrugged. "No particular reason. I just didn't figure he was the type of person they'd like and vice versa."

Cael didn't press for more details on the claim. "We were reviewing his most recent text conversations on his phone and we gathered that you steered him away from something. In an unsent draft, he told you that it was over and thanked you. Can you elaborate on that?"

Emmett gazed down at his hands, appearing to debate his answer, before he shook his head. "No, I don't know what that would've meant. That's probably why he never sent it."

Minka decided to shift the topic back to his

abduction. "Did you have any clues about where you were kept?"

"They kept a bag over my head most of the time, but I'm fairly certain it was a shed," he said, confirming their suspicions.

"And all they discussed with you was Logan?" Cael asked.

"Yes."

Maxed out of questions, the detectives wished him a quick recovery and departed. On the ride home, they concluded that whatever operation Logan was hiding must've been what led to both his murder and Emmett's abduction and torture.

"Do you suppose they found out about that message Logan drafted to Emmett?" Minka questioned Cael.

"How?"

"They could've cloned his phone and spied on everything he did. Then, they made their move when he showed himself to be a traitor." Another scenario occurred to her. "I still think they followed him off the ship. It's the only way this all makes sense."

"But it doesn't make sense that they'd steal a car and draw attention to themselves, instead of just driving their own."

"Maybe they wanted it to appear that they remained on board the ship. Plus, using someone else's vehicle allowed them to do their dirty work without anybody knowing who they were."

He nodded, but without any proof, they dropped the subject for now. Still, Minka continued to ponder what they could've been trying to protect. Logan's messages to both the superheroes and Emmett indicated that whatever he was doing had been ongoing, rather than a one-time act. The fact that he was at sea almost nonstop, combined with everything else, left little doubt in her mind that the operation had to be going on aboard *The Exquisite Marvel*.

Unable to scout out the ship until the next day, she resolved again to focus her day on her family. Gus Channing and his wife invited the whole Avery clan and a few others to their house for a barbecue and pool party that afternoon. Several friends and family members used the opportunity to pick on Minka about the baby's gender, with nearly everyone present in on the secret. She tried to be a trooper about it, but she grew tired of playing the punchline of all the jokes.

Gus's wife, Lola, went the easiest on her, the two sharing in casual conversation while Minka's friend made the hors d'oeuvres. As usual, however, the dynamic changed when Autumn, Cael's wife, joined them.

"So have you and Wes talked about baby names?" her sister-in-law questioned.

"Not at length yet. I'm sure he'll just taunt me when we do. It is a little awkward to discuss it in theoretical terms, when one of us knows the reality."

"I can't fathom how you can take waiting," Lola replied.

"Neither can I," Autumn agreed. "Remember how I drove everybody crazy with choosing a name before we learned Tyson was a boy? I thought I wanted the surprise, but I just needed that name and everything to visualize him and draw closer to him."

Minka said nothing, but the comment reminded her of the woman's remark at Lamaze class. She didn't like people questioning her relationship with her unborn, but the more she considered it, the more she began to doubt herself. She had to admit that she started picturing Caela the instant her gender was revealed, especially as she prepared her nursery and talked about her by name. She couldn't envision doing any of those with the new baby, making her wonder if their future relationship would reap further consequences.

Nonetheless, she tried to enjoy her evening. The gathering proceeded without a hitch, with the kids enjoying the Channing family's new in-ground pool. Typically in bed by the time they'd finished dessert, they were thrilled when their parents agreed to let them take another brief dip before they'd call it a night. In the meantime, Minka drifted away from the crowd, taking her second serving of dessert to a lonely lounge chair.

Before long, Wes meandered over. "There you are. Are you feeling okay?"

"I'm better now that I have this," she joked about her piece of cheesecake.

He chuckled but didn't fall for her diversion tactic. "You've been kind of quiet tonight."

"I've just been thinking. A couple of people have implied that I'm not going to be close to the baby because I don't know if it's a boy or a girl."

He took her hand and stroked it. "That's nonsense, honey."

"Is it? What if this is just the start of a distance we'll have between us for the years ahead? I'm doing everything so differently from when I had Caela. I'm not learning the sex and can't personalize the nursery. Then, I'll be back to work after three months and won't have the quality time I did with her. Am I setting us up for disaster?"

She struggled with the question for most of her pregnancy. After several lengthy discussions, she and Wes had determined that she couldn't financially leave the force once again. She'd almost been back for two years, but not having planned the addition to the family or the house, they hadn't yet saved enough to support another six-year hiatus. Though many mothers faced the same predicament, she still had trouble accepting it.

"Sweetheart, anyone would be out of their mind to doubt your love for this baby," he assured her. "Your relationship is not going to depend on whether or not you learn the gender now."

"Maybe you should just tell me, though."

"No way! I am not letting anybody or even your hormones break the oath you made me take." His adamant declaration made her laugh. "But I don't think it'd be a bad idea if we revisited the name-choosing. I've been thinking about it, and we could go with a gender-neutral name. That way, we'll be on some common ground and can talk to this one by name."

"Did Robin call you, too?"

"Maybe, but I know you won't go for that." He snickered. "How about Peyton?"

"Peyton Avery—sounds like you gave it the athlete test." She chuckled, given he always considered how a name would appear on a scoreboard. She nodded in approval. "I like it."

He leaned in to kiss her and rested his hand on her stomach just in time to feel Peyton kick, seeming to endorse the name, as well. They smiled and greeted the little one by name for the first time, sharing a bonding moment the parents would remember always.

****

With *The Exquisite Marvel* not set to dock until late morning, Minka and Cael started their day at the precinct. They called forensics to discern if they'd collected anything of interest in the SUV or shed. First off, they confirmed that the blood on the hammer was, indeed, Emmett's, verifying that it was where he'd been kept. While their instinct about a lack of fingerprints had also been affirmed, there'd been sand particles on the carpet under the driver's seat of the vehicle. They pointed out, however, that it could've been from the owners.

Sadie had nothing to share on her end, so they used their time waiting to write up their reports on Emmett's abduction and recovery. Just after ten o'clock, they set out on their journey toward the Atlantic coast and arrived at Port Canaveral an hour later. They noticed the traffic became heavier as they approached the docks, leading to the presumption that several cruise liners had just returned to port. They hoped *The Exquisite Marvel* had been one of them as they climbed out of Cael's car and made their way to the boarding station.

Explaining the reason for their presence to security, Minka and Cael walked through the winding hallways to the port. A few oncoming passengers gazed at them in confusion due to their lack of luggage. Minka couldn't help but become nostalgic, with the experience reminding her of her and Wes's journey through those same corridors as newlyweds. They'd been filled with excitement, as the dawn of their honeymoon ushered in anticipation over the start of their new life together.

Minka sprang out of her wistful state, however, the instant they boarded the ship. They flashed their badges several more times along the way, but the ship sat nearly empty of crew workers. Thus, they had to rely on the security staff to guide them to Logan Baris's cabin. The vacant halls showed no promise of them being able to talk with any of his colleagues, so they were both shocked and thrilled to meet his roommate behind the door.

"Oh, I'm sorry, Wynn. We didn't reckon anybody was in here," the guard apologized to him. "These detectives are investigating Logan's murder."

Clearly grieving, the young man acknowledged it with a nod. "It's not a problem. I was just waiting around to see if Luca, his brother, was coming aboard to collect his belongings. I can get out of your way. I appreciate whatever you need to do to identify whoever's responsible for this. Logan was a good friend."

"Actually, we'd like you to stick around and give us some insight into his final days," Cael told him. "You guys were pretty close?"

He nodded. "I was hired a month or so before him, and I wasn't keen on having a roommate. We hit it off right away, though, and never really had any problems. We even took a couple of trips together."

Minka noted the contrast from the cruise director's previous claim about Logan's lack of socializing. "Did everybody else seem to get along with him well?"

"I'd say so. Sure, when you're together as much as we all are, you're bound to have a spat here and there but nothing major."

"The last time you saw him was probably Wednesday, right?" Cael asked.

"Yes. He told me something urgent was going on, and he needed to get home."

"Was that all he told you?" Minka inquired.

Wynn sighed and nodded again. "I tried getting more out of him, but he wouldn't budge. He said I was better off not knowing."

Minka recognized the similarities between his narrative and Emmett's, even if Emmett portrayed Logan's personality a bit bleaker. "Had you noticed changes in his behavior recently?"

"He seemed to be gone more than usual, but everyone's busy. Thinking back, I guess he was a bit quieter, too, in the past few weeks."

The detectives took his input into consideration and were about to conclude the interview when Minka noticed a superhero emblem hanging above his bed. It reminded her of the contacts in Logan's phone. "You a big comic books fan?"

"Yeah, I'm not ashamed to label myself a nerd," Wynn admitted with a childlike grin. "Logan was, too. That was one of the reasons we bonded so quickly. He arrived with his collection, and I had one, too. We were debating which creator was better before we even learned each other's name."

Minka observed his spirits beginning to lighten, and she almost regretted having to keep the tone serious. "I hope those discussions never became heated."

He gave her a perturbed sidelong glance. "We were both pretty passionate, but it didn't turn violent, if that's what you're asking."

With Wynn being their best resource at the moment, Cael eased up on him. "We found several superhero-themed contacts listed in Logan's phone. Would you happen to know who those people may be?"

"Not at all. He never mentioned that to me. I guess one could've been me."

"May we see your phone?" Minka asked.

When he handed it over without reservation, she figured there was nothing incriminating on it. Otherwise, he would've insisted they get a warrant or at least hesitated. She scrolled through his messages, but it didn't feature any of the exchanges they'd viewed on Logan's. Of course, he could've deleted them since or used another phone, but his next statement made her doubt that was the case.

"I hardly use it since we don't have cell service at sea. We have Wi-Fi, but it isn't great."

Minka believed him since a quick search showed he'd made no calls and sent only a few texts since the ship's latest departure. For good measure, Cael took the phone from her and accessed his conversation history with Logan and scanned through the infrequent, ordinary messages between the roommates. Once finished, he regarded Minka, who shrugged, and gave the phone back to its owner.

Wynn accepted it. "As much as I want to help, I have some appointments lined up since we have a couple of days off before we set out again. Is that okay?"

They excused him and expressed their appreciation for his assistance. Before he wandered off, Minka posed one last question, "Do you guys leave your vehicles in the garage here during your voyages?"

He wore a puzzled expression and shrugged. "Some do, and others don't. We don't have to pay, but the space can be tight. Plus, you run the risk of theft. A lot of us use ride-sharing apps or take a bus."

Cael and Minka shared a look, then wished him well. His departure permitted them to examine Logan's belongings in private. At first glance, his side of the cabin appeared untouched, offering little of interest to Minka and Cael. It wasn't much of a surprise, given they'd recovered his phone and tablet at his residence, but it was aggravating nonetheless. Despite their conversation with Wynn, the trip seemed rather worthless.

As their search wound down, Cael stumbled on a revelation. "Didn't Wynn say Logan brought a collection of comic books on board with him?" When Minka substantiated his memory, he continued, "Have you seen any?"

"You think he took them home with him?"

"We should check because those can be valuable. The rare ones are worth thousands."

She grinned. "I trust you've looked?"

"I may have attended a conference or two after I graduated from the academy," he admitted. "My point is, if his set was good enough, it could've been stolen or even led to his death."

"You're implying somebody may have committed murder for a few magazines with drawings of men in tights?"

Cael scowled at her. "How dare you say that while you're carrying my niece or nephew!"

Minka rolled her eyes and continued to scope around the cabin for anything they might have missed. They were ready to leave when another young man entered the cabin. His clear resemblance to Logan said he was obviously the victim's brother.

"Who are you two?" Luca Baris greeted them, his tone agitated.

"Detective Avery, Orlando PD." Cael shook Luca's hand. "We talked Friday on the phone. My partner and I just decided to come out and see if we could make any headway."

Luca accepted his explanation and shared that he was there to pick up his brother's possessions, as Wynn had anticipated. The three engaged in small talk, with the detectives expressing their sympathies again and confessing that they had yet to discover a major lead. Aware his time was limited and that he would appreciate some privacy during the difficult task, they tried to be brief, but Cael followed through on satisfying his curiosity. "Wynn commented on your brother's collection of comics, but we haven't spotted a trace of it. Do you know where it'd be?"

"It's under his bed, just like it has been since he was eight," Luca claimed with certainty. Having already searched there, Minka and Cael allowed him to check, but he made the same realization they had. "That's strange. Maybe he took it with him, but that would've been quite a task. He has over two-hundred comics."

Minka was flabbergasted. "And he brought them all here?"

Luca had to chuckle. "I tried to persuade him not to, but he wouldn't have it. They were very special to him because most belonged to our dad."

Cael let a moment pass out of respect. "So, he probably wouldn't have sold them, huh?"

"Not even if he was flat broke."

****

On their way back to Orlando, Minka and Cael stopped by Logan's apartment to try to locate the missing comic book collection. Rummaging through all of his effects, they still didn't locate a single one, let alone two hundred. They retired exasperated but somewhat enlightened at the same time. They considered it a big deal for something so expansive and valuable to mysteriously vanish, especially only days after Logan's death. Of course, it begged the question of whether it was taken before or after he disembarked the ship. One thing grew ever clearer, though—the superheroes' names in his phone had to be more than innocent aliases.

After they exited the building, Cael called Emmett's hospital room to determine whether he'd spotted them anywhere. He corroborated Luca's claim, stating Logan always stored it on-board. To their gratitude, however, he divulged some information they didn't elicit.

"I was speaking with a psychiatrist and remembered something my abductors said during our scuffle. One told the other he should've brought the drugs."

The statement reawakened Minka's theories about Logan being involved in drug smuggling, and she didn't hesitate to circle back to it the instant Cael hung up. "Now, do you deem a drug operation as a viable possibility?"

"I guess I have to. I just can't believe it could go unnoticed on a major cruise-line like this. Why would they want Emmett to overhear such an admission?"

"With him as beaten as he was, they probably didn't think he'd absorb it, and he didn't right away." She mulled it over, trying to untangle all the knots in this complex net. "We should've explored the ship further. Whatever he had cooking must've been occurring there."

"But I'm sure Logan traversed the whole vessel every day. How could we narrow down where to look? We'd get nowhere by requesting access to wherever the secret drug stash is hidden."

With their resources regarding his life at sea so

limited, they had to make full use of what they had. Thus, she sought out his social media pages once they returned to the precinct. A plethora of photos showed him with fellow crew members and even some passengers. In browsing through them, Minka couldn't help but wonder if any of these smiling faces could've been his partner in crime and his killer. The endless feed made it seem like an impossible feat to figure out, but suddenly, she noticed a familiar tattoo on a man whom Logan had coined as one of his *favorite travelers.*

She swiveled her screen around to share it with her brother-in-law at the opposite side of their shared desk and maximized the image. "Recognize this?"

Leaning in closer, he examined the body ink on the guy's neck which showed the outline of an eagle with the number three in Roman numerals inside it. "Well, well, well. If it isn't Thiago Fontanilla, one of Florida's most notorious drug lords."

Chapter Four

After months of eluding authorities, Thiago Fontanilla had been apprehended that winter and was in a jail cell, awaiting his trial. The photo on Logan's social media page was posted the previous October when Fontanilla's drug business was alive and thriving. The idea of him being on a professional vacation was anything but far-fetched. With his face and unique tattoo plastered all through Florida for nearly a year before that, it'd be hard to believe Logan was unaware of his reputation. The only baffling element to the situation was why security had allowed him on the ship in the first place, instead of handing him over to the FBI.

While the felon couldn't speak for them, Minka and Cael hoped to get answers out of him concerning his relationship with Logan. Thus, they paid a visit to the correctional institution in Clermont. During the forty-five-minute trek, they speculated the ways he could've coerced the cruise ship worker into his exploits and how that could've resulted in his demise. They understood full well that when dealing with operations like drug trafficking, detaining the main man wasn't the end of the organization. After all, he'd had enough time to round up recruits, and Logan could've been one of them. When he decided to back out, Fontanilla could've sent two of his other pawns to his door. Whether or not they were crewmates of his, the detectives endeavored to figure out.

Once at the reformatory, a guard led Minka and Cael to the interrogation room, where Fontanilla was escorted several moments later. The instant he sat down, an arrogant sneer crossed his lips, indicating it wouldn't be an easy interview.

"Detectives Avery, I'm told." He gazed at Minka's stomach against the table and gestured to it with his handcuffed arm. "Looks like you two mixed business with pleasure."

Not bothering to clear up the misconception about her and Cael's relationship, Minka transitioned swiftly to the task at hand. "It seems you have a lot of experience with that, too."

"Oh, you're that deaf cop in Orlando." He changed the subject with ease. "It's a pleasure. You know, you inspired me to give crime a try, since law enforcement clearly isn't what it used to be."

"Then, why am I the one with the badge and you're the one with the handcuffs?" she replied, unfazed. "As much as I appreciate hearing from my fans, we're here to discuss your last cruise as a free man. Do you remember this photo being taken?"

Fontanilla eyeballed the image. "Sure. He was a cool dude. He has a great voice for punk rock."

"How familiar did you get with him?" Cael inquired.

Fontanilla's haughtiness decreased a notch, and his face displayed genuine confusion. "That's the extent of it, bro. My lady friend and I enjoyed his performance and caught up with him for a picture."

"Even you big-time drug lords get star struck, huh?" Minka replied.

"I wouldn't go that far. The guy's just a cabaret

singer. What's this all about, anyway?"

"He was killed on Thursday, and we wondered if you knew anything about it," Cael informed him.

"Why should I? He just worked on a cruise I was on eight months ago. Considering what I've gone through since then, he's the last person on my mind."

"You can't expect us to believe you went on that cruise purely for relaxation," Minka said.

"Why not? I work as hard as you two do, so I need a break on occasion."

Cael folded his arms. "You didn't use the opportunity to tie up some loose ends or maybe recruit new help?"

"No. My girl and I merely needed some alone time. When you're an entrepreneur like me, you don't get much time for romance."

"Probably because you're always running from the law," she stated. "The sacrifices of a fugitive."

Cael made one more stand. "Is there anything unusual you recall about him or the cruise in general?"

"Nah, everything was pretty typical. There were a few cases of food poisoning, but we never had a problem. The older folks seemed to be more susceptible to it."

The detectives took a quick note of his observation but resented the fact that the tidbit was all they yielded from the interview. Just four days after the murder, it was already feeling like a cold case. Whether they wanted to face it or not, they were dealing with a victim whose life—and likely, troubles—stretched out of their jurisdiction, though his murder happened in it. Nonetheless, they couldn't merely deem the case unsolvable because of that, as they had a duty to mete out justice for Logan and stop whatever operation he tried to escape. If it was serious enough to kill over, it put countless others at risk, too.

With her mind frazzled by the time she made it home, Minka flinched upon opening the door and hearing Fritzi squawk. "Minka's home!"

She peered over at the bird in dismay, more disturbed by that phrase than the pregnancy one, particularly after she discovered both Wes and Caela were upstairs. Hearing her husband working in the nursery, she trotted up the steps in earnest.

"Please, tell me that bird heard you say I was home," she begged in desperation.

"No, she let me know. I was impressed."

"Well, I'm not." His wife shuddered inside over the image of Camille Paleta always watching for her to turn into the driveway.

Wes put his drill in his tool belt and crossed the room to kiss her. The two proceeded to discuss some of the day's developments in the case, as Minka related her and Cael's experience on *The Exquisite Marvel*. Sharing his brother's interest in comics, he was keenly intrigued by their quest for Logan's compilation. He, too, agreed it couldn't be coincidence, but he put a different spin on it than they'd considered.

"I understand why his brother doesn't want to believe he would sell them, but you didn't want to, either, when Robin sold your grandpa's watch."

"Robin's an exception. Plus, he was going on the run."

"Who's to say Logan wasn't in as dire of straights? You think he was involved in some kind of scheme, so it wouldn't be hard to imagine him being forced into desperate measures."

"It could've even been used as leverage to make him get or stay involved," Minka agreed. Observing him finish up his work, Minka glanced down at the nail gun lying on the floor beside her and retrieved it. "You could help Mama release some aggression."

Wes snickered. "You're welcome to add some reinforcement to the drywall. Just beware of the kickback."

"You married a cop, remember?" She aimed at the line of nails already fastened to the studs and fired the trigger, but nothing happened. "Am I out of ammo?"

Her husband grinned. "No, honey, you can't fire it like a pistol. It won't discharge unless it's against the object."

She followed his instruction, placing the tool up to the wall, and inserted the nail. "That's not as satisfying as I imagined."

"Why does that relieve me?" he teased.

She giggled until she noticed that the door didn't appear big enough for the opening. She trekked over to it, but Wes cut off her path. She raised the nail gun in jest. "I'm trained to use this now."

He stepped out of the way, hands up, but made his defense. "We're going to fix it."

She swung the door closed, but sure enough, a six-inch gap remained between it and the jamb. "This will be a dream when we're trying to get our newborn to sleep."

"Like I said, we're going to fix it. I gave Sal the wrong measurements, and neither of us realized it until we hung it. Guess we should've bought a pre-hung one."

Yeah, then the whole mechanism would've been wrong. Minka smirked but kept silent.

"He ordered the right size, and it'll arrive next week.

Fathers-to-be can get pregnancy brain, too," Wes told her.

A hungry Caela padded in, putting an end to their banter. As Minka drew out the pork chops Wes had baking in the oven, her mind drifted back to the case. She had to wonder if her theory about the comics being used as blackmail had any truth to it, and if so, how that could fit into what they'd already deduced. Logan wanted out of whatever was going on, so it'd make sense that, if his cohorts wanted to keep him around, they'd give him a reason to stay. She deemed it silly to fathom that comic books could be used as a hostage of sorts, but she reasoned it was probably his most prized possession— both in economic and sentimental value.

Along with that, she was struck by the possibility that this could've been his reason for fleeing the ship. He could've discovered the books were missing and frantically hurried to recover them. After all, he'd claimed to his boss that a family emergency had arisen, and if this were the case, it wouldn't have been an outright lie; perhaps the last memories he had of his father were snatched away from him.

Of course, the scenario would strongly suggest that whoever was trying to manipulate him had to be on *The Exquisite Marvel*, as well. That's the only way anyone would've had access to the collection, under the assumption that he still stowed it on-board with him. The more Minka pondered it, the better sense the notion made. Like Wynn admitted, the crew was together almost all the time. He'd have much more opportunity to get tangled up in exploits with his companions there, rather than ones he hardly associated with at home.

The whole situation worsened her desire for more

time with the ship's crew and her ire that their resources were so limited. The ship docked just once every five days, taking all of the potential suspects with it when it embarked on a new voyage. True, they could employ the help of the Brevard County Sheriff's Office, which oversees the port, or even the Coast Guard, but neither would have the insight into the case she and Cael did.

Tuesday morning, Minka and Cael agreed they needed to consult with Gus. The captain listened to the series of setbacks over the previous few days and sympathized with their tough position.

"And his only relative around is his brother, whom he only visits once a year?" Gus tried to dig for any other sources they'd overlooked. After they nodded, he paused in contemplation. "Is there anyone else he was in close contact with, who may know what he was doing?"

"None we're aware of," Cael replied with a sigh. "He only called or texted these supposed superheroes, who've all disconnected their numbers. Other than that, there's his roommate, of course, who claims he's in the dark."

"These 'superheroes'—do you believe they were fellow crewmates?"

"I wouldn't rule it out," Minka informed him. "Most of his life was on that ship. To me, it only stands to reason any trouble he was up to took place there."

Gus rocked back in his seat, as he always did while contemplating. "And if it was, then it's out of our jurisdiction. That ship's on international waters, so anything that happens after it docks isn't even the country's duty. You guys just need to do what you can here to make sure our people are safe, even if you can't solve this murder. Meanwhile, I'll make some calls to the

Coast Guard and Border Patrol to alert them of our suspicions about a drug trafficking operation."

"Logan's roommate on the ship said they had a few days between voyages, so this would be the ideal time to scope it out," Cael said.

Minka agreed with his resolution, hoping the feds would uncover something. No detective wanted to accept a case going unsolved, and up to this point, she thankfully hadn't had to. Now that she was in Homicide, the possibility became greater, and deep down, she figured the day would come.

An hour later, Gus reported that Emmett's statement about the drugs didn't give Border Patrol or even the DEA enough to launch an investigation. Neither agency received any other tips about the ship or crew. Plus, Emmett's condition didn't give the claim much credence, and even assuming he was correct, the words were uttered on land by men who might not have any ties to the ship.

On their own yet again, Minka and Cael combed through Logan's phone for something that hinted to drugs or his secret, but the superheroes remained their only grounds for suspicion. With no leads emerging the rest of the morning, they took longer lunch breaks than usual. Minka spotted an issue of *The Miracle of Motherhood* magazine she'd bought at the café a few days ago and took it with her to peruse it, skimming an article on the latest nursery fashions. After she highlighted a couple of ideas, she flipped to the next write-up, which shared ways to enjoy your second trimester. With Cael seated across from her in the break room, she had to joke with him about it.

"Guess I'm not on trend. Chasing after killers isn't

'the thing to do' during my second trimester."

"Bogus article!"

She giggled, browsing through what she was supposed to be doing, including indulging in spa days and wellness classes. With the busy life she led, all of the luxurious suggestions amused her. When her eyes crossed the words "Take a Babymoon", she initially kept her cynicism intact, until an idea occurred to her. She put it down and told her partner, "I need a babymoon!"

****

"Of all the plans you've proposed, Minks, I swear..." Gus cried later that day.

"Like we told you, our resources are so limited. We need a look into the victim's life—as we do in every case. Going undercover is the only way to get it," Minka told him in her defense.

"And like I told you, this isn't your job. Your job is to uncover everything you can about his life here and whether or not an element of it led to his death. Whatever transpired at sea is out of our hands."

"As well as our jurisdiction," Cael added.

Unwilling to give up on her idea, she inquired, "Suppose I, hypothetically, just wanted a vacation, and I just so happened to book a cruise on *The Exquisite Marvel*. During the voyage, what if I witnessed something that could be pertinent to a hypothetical investigation? Would you allow me to act on it, hypothetically speaking?"

"What you do in your hypothetical spare time is none of my business. However, you could only take legal action on American soil."

"Then, Cael and I need the rest of the week off, starting Thursday."

Cael's eyes widened. "We do?"

She said nothing, marching out of the office and up to her desk. She proceeded to get on her computer and go to the cruise line's website. "Would you rather an inside cabin or one with a balcony?"

"Have you lost it?" Cael questioned in sincerity. "Is this some sort of prenatal madness or what?"

"It's determination, Cael. We both became cops to get justice for people, regardless of jurisdiction. This may be our only chance to get it for Logan."

He didn't disagree with her but pointed out a vital flaw in her reasoning. "If these guys were from the ship, how can we be assured they're even onboard now? They clearly weren't when they dropped Emmett off at the rest stop."

"My guess is after they've ditched him, they'll go back to set sail again. It was perfect timing. Maybe they figured no one would notice their absence for one trip, but they would after two."

He crossed his arms, maintaining his cynical demeanor. "How do you propose we can even book this in a couple of days? Mom and Dad always have to secure their itineraries more than a year in advance."

"A friend of mine from high school is a travel agent. She's assured me before that a few cabins always open up because of last-minute cancelations, so she could get us a deal."

"Say we go through with this," he replied. "Do you really suppose my wife and your husband are going to take kindly to the idea of us going on a romantic cruise, posing as a loving mother- and father-to-be?"

"Why wouldn't they? You and I are like bickering siblings. They know that. Plus, we've all been married for years. We're secure in our own relationships."

He leveled a skeptical frown at her, and that evening, his doubts proved to be well-founded. The two families had dinner together at Wes and Minka's, after which Caela and Tyson played upstairs while the adults chatted. Minka and Cael discussed the difficulties of the case, leading up to her proposition. As they proceeded, Wes and Autumn grew very silent until Cael finished.

"Nothing's set in stone, but if we do this, we'd be leaving Thursday," Minka stated.

"Just the two of you?" Autumn questioned.

"In the same cabin?" Wes added.

"How would it appear if I requested a separate room from the father of my child?" Minka asked him.

"About as disturbing as it looks for you to leave him for a week to take a babymoon with his brother!" he argued. "Scoop already thinks Caela is Cael's, as it is."

"Caela is Cael's! Caela is Cael's!" Fritzi echoed.

"Nice going," Minka told her husband.

"Well, honey, you can't expect me to happily just agree to my pregnant wife going on vacation with another guy, even if it is my little brother."

"Ditto…to everything except the pregnant part," Autumn said.

"Come on, guys." Minka stayed the course. "If I had wanted him, I would've gone after him a long time ago. We would take you both, but it's so risky. We don't know what we're facing, and having two extra people could make us more noticeable."

Autumn maintained her stance. "Or it could help you blend in. A lot of couples take trips like this in groups. You guys tagged along on mine and Cael's babymoon. We'd simply be two sets of in-laws, enjoying the experience together, like we did in Jamaica."

"And I'd be your baby daddy," Wes told his wife. "And your stunt double, if needed."

"Now, the truth comes out: You just want in on the action," Minka accused him.

"None of this was my idea!"

Staying on topic, Cael rejoined the debate. "I like Autumn's thought. We can still keep our eyes peeled, and if we sense anything, we'll disappear for a while—without either of you following us. Is that clear?"

All of them glared at Wes, who meekly nodded.

"Who's going to watch Tyson and Caela, though?" Autumn asked.

"Caela is Cael's!" the bird sang.

She pointed to the cage. "And that?"

"Camille should be back for her the morning we leave," Wes said. "As for the kids, I'm sure Mom and Dad will be happy to babysit."

"Then, I guess it's, 'Bon voyage,' to us," Autumn declared with a smile.

****

With the cabins booked and their itinerary set, Minka and Cael still had one day of work to continue to glean what they could on Logan. Their hopes were high for their impromptu business trip, but they couldn't waste the whole day packing their suitcases. There was a chance all of this would prove to be in vain, in which case Minka would be too embarrassed to return to work. She wanted to leave with the assurance that they'd tried their best to solve the case before resorting to such questionable measures.

On her way to the precinct, Minka decided to swing by the morgue to touch base with Sadie. Not having heard from her since Monday, she doubted the medical examiner had anything to share, but she figured it didn't hurt to check.

The two arrived at the same moment, and Sadie exited her car first to unlock the building. As she strode toward her friend, Minka noticed that, in the five days since they'd seen each other, the expectant mother had grown rounder.

"I'll have to tell Caela you've popped a few extra kernels now," she teased.

"Tell me about it. I just ordered new scrubs. I suppose it's about time. We're six months today."

"I could only wish to have stayed in my clothes for that long." Minka chuckled. "I wanted to drop over and ask if you've made any breakthroughs in our victim's cause of death."

"Actually, I have. I was going to call you last night, but I had to rush off for my checkup. I told you his lungs were in bad shape, which I originally attributed to smoking. I put some tissue under the microscope yesterday, though, and it looked more like pulmonary edema, which is a build-up of fluid in the lungs. A number of conditions could've caused it, like a heart problem or pneumonia. It could've also resulted from chest trauma."

"But it wasn't triggered by the gunshot?" Minka asked.

"I've examined my share of gunshot victims and those of violence but have never run across damage like this. I haven't spotted signs of a struggle, either. I'm going to have a colleague come over and examine the lung tissue. I'll update you on his read on it."

"We appreciate it, but it may be hard getting ahold

of us. We're all going on a cruise—actually, the one where Logan worked. We're sort of mixing business with pleasure, and we'll see where it leads."

Sadie smiled. "Nice, undercover work in the Caribbean."

"I've had worse assignments. I'm sorry you'll be out a Lamaze partner Saturday."

"No worries. I wanted to take Jed, anyway. They're discussing labor pains, so I figure it'd serve him well to get a glimpse into his wife's suffering." They both chuckled. "Did Dr. Bailey sign off on your trip?"

"I didn't think she had to. Should I have checked?"

"Well, all I know is I wanted to go to my cousin's wedding in September, but she cautioned me against it. Technically, we're allowed to fly up until nine months, but she advises stopping at eight. With you only being five and travelling by boat, there's probably no problem. Then again, yours is a geriatric pregnancy, so…"

"Do not say the 'g' word," Minka warned her, very opposed to being associated with the term at only thirty-five. "I'll give her a call."

Thanking her for the information, she headed for the station, on edge the whole way about whether she could go on the cruise for which she so heartily begged—and paid. The last-minute 'deal' wasn't exactly a price buster, and since it was a mere two days away, the guys had opted against travel insurance. Considering the ticket was already in her name, it'd be hundreds of dollars wasted if she couldn't use it.

Since the doctor's office didn't open for another hour, she ran an Internet search on the matter. Twenty-four weeks was the cut-off mark, affording her a two-week window. Still, the experts advised each woman to consult her doctor, especially in cases of geriatric pregnancy. As soon as ten o'clock struck, Minka dialed the number, frantic. She explained the predicament to the receptionist, who then transferred her to the obstetrician directly. The doctor assured her that she and the baby were both in fine condition to go, and she wished her patient a good time.

With that anxiety gone, Minka focused back on work. She updated Cael on Sadie's latest discovery, and he agreed with the notion that Logan's lung damage hadn't occurred through natural means. What they couldn't agree on, however, was why the culprits would use such a method to kill him.

"Maybe he was part of an experiment, and something went wrong," Minka said. "They could've paid him for it, explaining his mysterious profits, and maybe this last time was when he started feeling the deadly side effects. That could be the drugs the kidnappers referenced around Emmett."

"I doubt that his busy schedule would allow him to play a lab rat, Minks."

She concurred with him on that, but then, another troubling scenario occurred to her. "What if this was happening on the ship? What if it's terrorists prepping for biochemical warfare? Cael, we're going on that cruise. If our cover is blown, what if the criminals use it on us?"

"Slow down," he counseled. "If anyone had biochemical weapons on board, why wouldn't they use them on Logan right there? It would've saved them from having to steal a car and commit kidnapping."

She contemplated the possibility and soon arrived at the same conclusion. Their colleague, Dawson Michaels, approached their desk a few minutes later. A crime analyst, Dawson graduated from the police academy with Minka, and like her, he stepped away from law enforcement for several years in the best interests of his family. He still only worked at the precinct part-time, running a diner during his civilian hours.

"Hey, guys." Dawson plopped his tablet down on the desk. "Captain Channing filled me in on your case involving the cruise ship worker. I did some digging and noticed that four passengers have been reported missing from *The Exquisite Marvel* in the past year. Thankfully, three ended up catching a flight home after the ship departed without them, but one is still missing. The FBI is in charge of the investigation, but they haven't made progress for the last seven months."

"Then, why did the Coast Guard tell Gus they hadn't received any other alerts about it?" Cael questioned.

"Unfortunately, it's not unusual for people to get stranded," Dawson replied. "They lose track of time or get plastered—usually both, a lot of times—and miss the boat, as they say."

Minka nodded. "On our honeymoon, they kept naming stragglers before we left the ports-of-call, in hopes they would report if they came aboard without swiping their boarding pass. We often wondered whether some of them made it in the end."

"This may be just another instance like that, but I figured I'd give you a heads-up, especially since you'll be on it." After they thanked him, he shifted toward Minka. "Once you get back, my wife has some clothes and toys our quads have outgrown now. They're an assortment of boys' and girls' stuff, so we're not spoiling your mystery."

Minka grinned. "I appreciate that."

He winked. "But Sadie's on stand-by for anything you figure out you don't need."

She swung back her head, not missing yet another hint to a son in her future. "I expected better from you, of all people."

He snickered and moseyed away. She transferred her focus from the tip about that to the one he offered regarding the case. The missing people, along with her speculation about bioweapons, rattled her confidence in her plan, with all of the unknowns amassing in her brain. She almost confessed her anxieties to Cael, but she restrained her tongue, realizing it wouldn't do more than create a ruckus. Hence, she endeavored to channel her nervousness into excitement.

On her way home from work, she took a brief detour to the mall, given her vacation wardrobe was all in her pre-baby sizes. Although Wes charged her with having enough maternity clothes for three more pregnancies, she figured a few more cruise-worthy pieces wouldn't be overboard. As she soon discovered, however, her husband had no right to scold her for her shopping spree, having gone on one of his own.

She entered their bedroom to put her purchases away, when in her peripheral vision, she spotted a dreadlocked stranger in the bathroom. Instinctively, she grabbed her weapon from her holster and pointed it at him. "Freeze!"

Wes whipped around and put his hands up. "You are way too distrusting."

"What is that on your head?" she demanded.

"It's my cover. I'm an orphan who was born in the islands and kidnapped by my pirate parents. Through the wonders of a DNA website, I recently discovered it and am on a mission to find my birth family before our baby is born. I'm trying to decide if 'Rico' or a 'Leandro' suits me better. What do you think?"

"I'd say 'El Crazo' would be more fitting!"

"Fine, if you don't like that, I have another option." He closed the door momentarily. When it reopened, he still wore the wig, but he placed the FBI hat Gus had bought him over it. "Kamole Onaona, Hawaiian FBI. They based a character off of me in one of those crime dramas." He winked before he took off the cap and examined it. "Why am I just now finding this?"

"Because I knew this would happen." His wife put her bags, which she'd dropped because of being startled, on the bed and shook her head. "Why can't you be content with enjoying a trip with your wife before we become parents of two and can barely remember each other's names?"

"Excuse me, but you showed no interest in doing so with *your husband* until this case arose. Even then, I wasn't part of your original plan."

It was the first time she perceived his pain over the night before, and guilt overtook her for being so insensitive to his feelings. She'd told him years earlier that no case was more important to her than he was, but in this instance, she hadn't conveyed that. Thus, she crossed the room and put her arms around him, trying to make up for hurting him.

"Honey, I was only thinking in realistic terms, as well as for your protection. It terrifies me to think of losing you, or worse yet, Caela losing one or both of us. My job almost cost us everything once already, and I'd hate to repeat that, with our daughter being the most affected. The safety of our family was all that lay behind my initial instinct. I never wanted to exclude you. I'm very much looking forward to some alone time in between hunting for bad guys."

His eyebrow shot up. "Does that mean I can take the wig?"

"For the cabin only." She winked, then kissed him.

Chapter Five

By the morning of their departure, exhausted from the preparations, Minka hankered for a vacation. She'd done the brunt of the packing—since, as Wes explained, the majority of the luggage belonged to her—and made numerous trips up and down the stairs due to forgetting things. Between pregnancy brain, along with her additional needs as a mother-to-be, she could already tell her little one wasn't going to give her a completely relaxing break from parenthood.

As for her other child who'd stay behind, Caela didn't make things easy, either. Never having been away from them for more than a night, she bawled the entire night before about being separated for almost a week. They let her sleep in their bed to compensate, but Minka's guilt remained. She'd tried so hard to assure the little girl of her unwavering love prior to the baby's arrival. She couldn't help but consider her efforts worthless now while she gazed at her sobbing child.

Despite the chaotic morning, Minka had everything packed with time to spare, during which she hoped to share a few tranquil moments with her daughter. In an hour, they were set to meet Cael and Autumn at Wes's parents' house, where the kids would be staying. To her displeasure, the brief respite became briefer when an all too familiar knock tapped on the door.

"Hello, hello!" Camille Paleta greeted, making her

bird sing with excitement.

"Someone's glad you're back," Minka stated, mentally following it up with, *And it isn't me!*

The older woman, who clearly had her red hair brightened during the getaway, approached the cage and gushed over her pet. Fritzi only grew louder and shriller. She hoped the commotion would shorten the visit.

"I can't thank you all enough. I hope she wasn't too much of a bother."

"She wasn't," Caela assured her, which Minka appreciated.

As the parrot continued to squawk, Camille seemed to hasten her exit, but her nosiness stopped her in her tracks upon noting the suitcases beside the stairs. "Looks like we aren't the only travelers this week. Where are you guys headed?"

"The Caribbean. We're taking a cruise before the little one comes with his or her own plans."

"Is it safe?" she demanded, her eyes big. "I mean, this baby seems to be in a hurry."

Only to get you to leave with your psychotic bird! "The doctor gave us the thumbs-up."

Camille still seemed cynical, but she stayed quiet for a change. She made her way out the door, but before exiting, she bent over and embraced Caela. "Enjoy swimming in the ocean, sweetheart."

"I'm not going on the cruise. I'm staying with my nana and papa," she replied matter-of-factly, making her mother cringe.

"You are? Well, it's nice of your grandparents to take care of you when Mommy and Daddy have more fun things to do," Camille said, her voice sweet to disguise her sour words.

Thankfully, Caela didn't seem to register the woman's true implication, and Minka wished her a good day—albeit between gritted teeth. She strived to shake off the rude remark, but it definitely robbed her of excitement for their impending journey. She had enough remorse piercing her, without someone essentially calling her the worst mother of the year.

"I wouldn't go that far," Wes corrected her when she said as much to him while they packed the car. He'd listened to the conversation from the kitchen, where he hid.

"I would. I'm putting my unborn child in danger by going when I'm apparently ready to burst, and I'm abandoning my other one to party."

He embraced her and assured her that she was a wonderful mother. His words comforted her, but what meant more was Caela's building anticipation for spending time with her grandparents and cousin. Nonetheless, Minka cried when she had to kiss her little girl goodbye, as Autumn did with nearly-two-year-old Tyson. For half of their drive, Minka was even contemplating how she could've snuck her on board.

Upon nearing the port, her emotions settled. With traffic busy, the four weren't able to park as close as Cael and Minka were on Monday, making for a long walk with a hefty load of luggage. Wes handled their bigger suitcase, while she carried the small overnight bag that held her selection of shoes. Once again, she couldn't help but reminisce about her and Wes embarking on their honeymoon as they weaved through the line to board.

Seeming to read her thoughts, her husband took her by the hand and gave her a tender look. "It's crazy how little has changed in twelve years. Here we are, side by side. I'm still in awe that the universe thought enough of me to let me marry the only girl I ever wanted to and become father to her children."

She gave his hand an appreciative squeeze, touched that he continued to feel that way about her. For that moment, she forgot all about the case and their purpose for the trip, happy to be with the man she loved.

The romance soon faded away, when they had to go through security. Minka was given an unusual amount of attention, being frisked even after passing through the metal detector without incident. The TSA agent focused on her stomach, until she surprised him by dryly telling him it was real. He smirked and released them on their way.

They entered through a passage different from the one the detectives used before and handed over their tickets before they stepped into the luxurious foyer. With red carpet beneath them and diamond chandeliers hanging from the mirrored ceiling, *The Exquisite Marvel* truly lived up to its name. Their ocean view stateroom was just as breathtaking, even more beautiful than it appeared online. The pale-yellow walls and furniture enhanced the sunlight peeking through the window, creating a stunning contrast to the blue of the sea.

Wes gave way to wishful thinking. "Gus is paying for this, right?"

His wife offered him a sidelong glance. "If he were, we'd all be in the boiler room."

After unpacking a few of their necessities, Minka had just decided to lie down for a brief while when the emergency alarms began to ring, signaling the usual safety drill. Thus, everyone collected their lifejackets and took the stairs to the top deck, where they were assigned to evacuate in the event of a real crisis. Minka had trouble from the get-go, as her life preserver would barely fit around her body.

"I'm a goner if worse comes to worse."

"It won't," Wes assured her.

"Need I remind you why we're here?" she whispered.

He chuckled and kissed her cheek. She paid astute attention to the crew workers, who were also gathered on the deck for the emergency drill. Unable to give them more than a casual glance, she didn't make any notable observations, other than their goofing off on the job.

After the exercise ended, they headed back to the cabin. While they strolled, they passed the first-aid room. Minka paused and motioned toward it, telling her family, "We'd better keep this in mind, just in case. I sure hope I don't become as acquainted with it as I did on our honeymoon."

Autumn winked and gave her a playful nudge. "Dare we ask what put you in there?"

She giggled, her cheeks warm. "I thought I had a chronic case of seasickness, but I turned out to be pregnant. We were married before the school year ended and didn't get away right after our wedding, so at least we weren't newlyweds in the fullest sense. My constant nausea didn't make the most romantic atmosphere."

"To be fair, romantic atmospheres were what put us in that position," Wes said.

She shook her head, embarrassed. Taking one more glance in the room, she reminisced on her days as a bride, which didn't seem that long ago…

She remembered staggering out of her and her groom's cabin, beyond sick for the third night in a row.

Being a first-time cruiser, she'd been queasy from the moment they set sail from Cape Canaveral. She spent their first morning hugging the toilet, and though Wes wanted to comfort her, the older ship's tiny bathroom only lent room for one.

Through it all, he and Minka both tried to be troopers. Her nausea quelled occasionally, allowing them to enjoy the honeymooners' experience to a degree. After they docked in St. Thomas the day before, her nausea abated for the most part, and they took pleasure in exploring the island together.

When her seasickness returned with a vengeance, however, she couldn't stay in the stuffy cabin for the rest of the evening. If her condition was headed where she feared it was, she hated to awaken her husband once again, losing ever more dignity. She hoped the fresh night air would give her some relief, but once she reached the top deck, the sight and motion of the rolling waves just worsened her symptoms.

Thus, she made her way to the first-aid room for the seventh time of the voyage. She and the night doctor, Trixie Campbell, had become well-acquainted during her frequent visits, both familiarized with each other's background to the point of knowing their family members' names. A middle-aged widow from Ireland, the doctor ironically had a deaf son, who, like Minka, had a cochlear implant put into his ear when he was young.

You, again? Dr. Campbell signed.

Yes, Minka gestured her fist. Uneager to move any more than necessary, she opted to say out loud, "I think I need another seasickness patch."

"You haven't even been wearing that one for an

entire day," the doctor protested, consulting her watch. "These usually last a good three."

"Well, I must have a defective one. It seemed to help for a while, but once we went to bed, it took hold again."

"A honeymooner's dream!"

"Tell me about it." She returned the sarcasm. "If only Wes had taken me to Paris, like I'd asked."

The older woman chuckled, putting on her plastic gloves before she removed the patch from behind Minka's ear. She kept quiet as she prepared a new one, but she eventually asked, "How's your appetite been through all of this?"

"When I can hold something down, I enjoy it. Wes has been teasing me about my making good use of the round-the-clock buffet."

Dr. Campbell nodded with a grin. "You've been married six weeks, correct?"

Minka nodded. "As of yesterday."

The doctor took off her gloves and put away the patches. "I'm sorry, Minka, but I can't treat you for this. Fingers crossed, your morning sickness should go away after your first trimester."

To this day, Minka couldn't believe she hadn't discerned her pregnancy sooner. Though she ended up losing the baby weeks later, she still cherished the memory.

Wandering past the crewmates, she snapped back to the present and into detective mode, reminding herself that every moment could produce a lead. The task challenged her more than she expected, with nothing about this feeling like an investigation. It was all too easy, especially when she was this tired, to simply take in the beautiful surroundings and disengage from the real world.

Another opportunity to study the staff arose soon after they returned to their room, when an announcement invited them to go to the auditorium for a welcoming address. Designed to highlight what the week held in store, Spencer Franklin, the cruise director whom Minka and Cael had spoken to on the phone, had center stage for most of the assembly.

Franklin didn't make the best first impression on Minka, beginning the discourse by having all of the children vacate the room with the daycare staff. Several times, he encouraged the passengers to take full advantage of the on-board daycare service so they could enjoy the activities kid-free. She deduced he wasn't a family man, but at the same time, she reckoned his presentation appealed to many couples. For her part, though, it only made her miss her little girl more.

During the last few minutes of the session, Franklin introduced the rest of the crew one by one, piquing the detectives' interest. They frantically jotted down the workers' names on their brochures and did their best to get a good look at each of them. Meanwhile, their spouses gave them both a nudge to alert them to the nearby travelers sending them confused looks.

Taking to heart the warning, Cael and Minka strived to be less conspicuous and employ their good memories for the final handful of introductions. Wynn McCallum, Logan's cabin-mate, was among them, prompting the detectives to give each other the eye. They'd discussed the possibility of running into him and agreed to avoid him as much as they could help it. Although neither of them considered him a suspect, they feared he'd recognize them and expose their identities to his colleagues, even innocently.

Wynn proved to be the least of their problems, however, when Franklin introduced the next crewmate.

Wes gasped before the name was declared. "Is that...?"

"Miss Shantelle Brayden," Franklin announced.

****

"Of all the cruise ships in a twenty-mile radius, of course, we end up on the one with the ex-con who sent my husband into hiding," Minka muttered.

"Settle down, honey," Wes counseled.

With the ordeal happening before she entered the family, Autumn tried to keep up with the development. "So she was the professional cheerleader who graduated with Wes, right?"

Cael nodded. "They reconnected while we were investigating the abductions of basketball players on her team. It ended up being linked to an illegal gambling ring run by her mobster fiancé, and she lured Wes to send us on a bogus lead. She didn't anticipate he'd follow up on it himself."

"I'll take it from there," Minka stated, making Wes rub his temples. "She and her fiancé tried to kill him, making him have to flee for his life. Then, they almost shot me and Cael once we caught up with them."

"How nice it is to reminisce," her weary husband mumbled.

"And now, she shows up while we're investigating the murder of one of the crew members. That can't be coincidence. She's already proven she's capable of killing somebody who gets in her way."

"Slow down, Minks," Cael said from behind her.

"Why should I? She hasn't earned our trust. So,

she's out of jail and has a job. It doesn't mean she's changed. It just means she hasn't been caught again. Well, she has now! I say we cuff her before the ship even leaves port."

The words barely escaped her mouth when the boat's horn blew as the ship pulled away from the dock. Minka hissed in defeat.

"Cool it," her partner rebuked again. "We need evidence. I'll admit, it might be the start of what we came to do. We'll keep an eye on her when we can, but we have to stick to the plan—your plan, I must add."

She understood that he was right, but her emotions made it difficult to accept. The woman had all but robbed her and Wes's future for her own gain, and she would've taken their lives had circumstances allowed. With each second that passed, similarities between her past stunts and Logan's murder piled up in Minka's head, and she couldn't overlook them.

She willed herself to, however, at least for the moment. They were all assigned to the earlier dinner, to Minka and Peyton's delight, giving them only an hour to roam the ship. They decided to stroll up to the top deck for the Sail Away party. While it didn't provide much for the investigation's part, it gave Minka a chance to decompress from the shock of seeing Shantelle Brayden again. After some time on a comfortable lounge chair, laughing at Wes and Cael dance in a conga line, her spirits lightened.

The four headed right down to the dining room a few minutes before six, not stopping to change clothes. Dinner didn't call for formal wear that night, but the luxurious venue made them feel like bums in their casual attire. Rows of chandeliers hung above pristine white linen tablecloths, making the place settings sparkle. It was similar to the one Minka and Wes had dined in as honeymooners, but with the ship thirty years younger and nearly double the size, everything was more elaborate than she'd imagined.

As an usher escorted them to their assigned seats, her intimidation eased when she peered around and noticed that everyone else had opted for a casual ensemble, too. In a cruel twist of fate, they ended up sitting beside the most extravagantly dressed woman there. Donning a floor-length gown and substituting eyeshadow for glitter, Tula Hawkings shined almost as brightly as her surroundings.

"Good evening," she greeted them, her warm tone unlike the highbrow welcoming Minka expected. "Oh, I see we have a little cruiser on board, as well. I love babies! When will this one be arriving?"

Caught off guard by how abruptly the conversation had progressed, Minka felt compelled to take the chair beside her, a choice she'd regret in short order. "Early November."

"Enjoy it while you can, honey. Before you realize it, this one will be off on his or her own, not wanting you to even learn where." She sighed and rolled her eyes, revealing her trials, Minka assumed. "I'm Tula, by the way, and this is my husband, Stewart. Our friends call us Tu and Stew!"

She shook hands with the older, bearded gentleman across from his wife, who seemed more reserved than Tula. Likewise, Minka introduced Wes.

The woman continued to surprise her. "What's your accent? Russian?"

"Deaf Floridian," she had to joke, wondering if the

oblivious woman was for real.

"How exotic," Tula replied.

Minka could only guess whether she didn't understand or if it was her way of being polite. Whatever the case, she was glad when the bizarre exchange was interrupted by the arrival of the last couple to the table, Griffin and Janine Garrets. The friendly couple strolled around and introduced themselves to each of their fellow travelers, before taking their seats at the end of the table. Once settled, Griffin made clear that their later entrance didn't suggest a lack of eagerness.

Griffin sniffed the air. "Smells like the pappardelle with sautéed langostino tails and a side of hickory smoked salmon."

Wes gave him an impressed smile. "How many times have you been on here?"

"This is our first cruise," Janine replied with a grin and an eye roll. "He's just been studying the menu since the moment we booked it."

"What can I say? She was ogling over the pictures of the cabins and the ballroom, but I was focused on what really matters." Her husband patted his stomach. "After all, this is my retirement celebration. I gave the force thirty long years to get here."

"You're a cop?" Cael asked.

"A detective."

"So are Cael and Minka," Autumn told the table, making Minka tense.

"Really? Well, check you out! What department?" Griffin inquired.

"Homicide now, in Orlando," Minka stated, trying not to show her hesitancy.

"I was in Narcotics for the majority of my years with

the Newport News PD. I was among the first to head up the division, in fact. At the start of my career, we'd only come across a few cases here and there. It's become a real problem in the last couple of decades, though. "

Minka's brow raised in her partner's direction, as the comment reminded her of her theory about Logan's murder being tied to the drug cartel. He gave her his customary response, shaking his head cynically, but she still considered Griffin a potential asset.

"Stewy was with the FBI for a brief stint." Tula tried to trump them all. Her follow-up made Minka doubt her credibility. "Was that before or after you invented the Internet, darling?"

"After," he explained. "The crooked tycoon who stole it from me inspired me to go into law."

She caressed his hand to soothe his pain, while Minka struggled to suppress her giggles. The humor in it faded a smidge when the mischief maker in Wes compelled him to regale them with his phony career with the Bureau. "I served at the agency in Honolulu before I met Minka. I was abducted as a child by pirates, and that drove my passion for crime fighting. A producer is about to make a television series about it."

Really? You're going with both ridiculous cover stories? Minka signed to him across the table. Beside him, Cael tilted his head in befuddlement.

"Well, haven't we hit the jackpot at this table?" Janine exclaimed.

Tula doubled down on her husband's supposed accomplishments. All ended in tragic disappointments. His prom date with a rising pop star was sabotaged by a teen idol in the eighties. A few years later, his international peace prize fell through due to a technical glitch—of course, caused by the man who ripped away his idea of the Internet. Needless to say, everyone else stuffed their mouths full of food when their waiter finally served dinner.

As Griffin had predicted, the pasta dish was placed in front of them, and at first sight, it appeared delicious. Unfamiliar with the cuisine, Minka wasn't expecting the seafood flavor mixed in, and apparently, neither did her sister-in-law.

"Does anyone know if it's supposed to taste…fishy?"

"Langostino is from a squat lobster," Griffin told Autumn.

"Didn't you hear him say 'sautéed langostino *tails*'?" Cael reminded her.

The vegan made a sickened face and slid the plate aside to finish her salad. The entrée wasn't to Minka's liking, either, but Autumn's squirming enhanced its appeal. She just hoped history wouldn't repeat itself, with her in the bathroom the whole night like on their honeymoon.

On the other hand, the Chocolate Decadence Cake served for dessert did not disappoint, and everybody wore happy faces after savoring it. The ship's photographer had them pose for a picture on their way out of the dining room, after which they returned to the top deck to again keep an eye on the crew. Spotting no signs of suspicious activity, they decided to venture elsewhere.

After meandering through the ship for another hour or so, they grew tired of being on their feet. Still somewhat early, they began to debate which of the vast array of activities would provide an amusing evening and perhaps a lead.

"Why don't we hit the cabaret show?" Cael said. "The theater's not far, and it starts in fifteen minutes."

Minka and Autumn both agreed to the notion, but Wes offered some push-back. "I'm pretty beat, guys. I don't really feel like applauding mediocre performances tonight."

"But this would've been the act Logan sang in," Minka whispered. "These would've been the crewmates he spent most of his time with, no doubt. Good call, partner."

"Even so, it isn't like they'll be running any schemes during the show," Wes told her.

"At least, we can get eyes on them," she replied.

"Could we just take one night for some relaxation before you two get rolling?" Wes pled.

"We only have five days to do this, so we need to be efficient in narrowing down our best candidates who might know something. Besides, it'll be fun. We never get to do anything like this at home and especially won't after the baby comes."

He smiled and drew her close, revealing his ulterior motives. "Another activity falls into that category, my dear!"

Now aware of his agenda, Minka laughed and vowed to make it up to him. Wes acquiesced and followed Cael and Autumn's lead to the auditorium. The live entertainment proved better than most similar acts, though many of the show tunes featured weren't on the guys' playlists. After the first set, a new group of singers and dancers entered the act, with one in particular catching Minka's attention.

She recognized Shantelle just as easily the second

time around, and so did Wes and Cael. The three shared a look, but they didn't make a move in an effort not to evoke anybody's suspicion. In the years since they last saw her, Shantelle maintained her tiny physique. Given her short frame, she couldn't have gained much weight without it showing, so Minka reckoned she'd made good use of the prison gym. She styled her dark brown hair much like she did back then, as well, curling the long locks. She proved to be a double threat, coupling her dancing skills with her unexpectedly pleasant singing voice.

The group stayed quiet for the rest of the performance. Despite her jovial front, it was difficult for Minka's mind not to dwell on the last time she spoke with the woman. After they detained Shantelle and her mobster fiancé, Tony DeSoto, in Phoenix, they all flew back to Orlando, where they interviewed the two from a holding cell. Before she and Cael spoke with her in a professional capacity, she insisted on having a one-on-one with the conspirator for her own satisfaction.

She could still envision the woman's glower of contempt and hear her clipped tone…

"I hear congratulations are in order," Shantelle greeted her from across the table, in handcuffs, referring to her pregnancy.

"Yes, I have my husband back, a baby on the way, and I helped take down the next dynasty of criminals before you two could start a life together. I'm not going to lie, it's been a good couple of days."

Shantelle gifted her a fake smile. "I'm happy for you. Meanwhile, my engagement's over and here I am, in a holding cell, paying for a crime my ex-fiancé engineered."

"That's why dating a mobster isn't on too many girls' bucket list," Minka replied.

"But I'll never get another diamond like that," she whined.

"Well, my ring may not be that massive, but I can relate. Until yesterday, I was pregnant and alone, terrified to face being a single mother. And this was all because of what you've done. You forced my husband out of our home, away from his family and everything he loves…and all out of greed. My child was going to have to live without a father because of a stupid gambling ring. Does that even matter to a shallow person like you?"

"Only if you're having a boy." Shantelle sneered. "I always envisioned having a son with Wes."

The memory had haunted Minka for weeks afterward, as something in her tone of voice and expression made her believe the felon was contriving a scheme against her. When she'd had to testify against her in court, Shantelle's glares at her pregnant belly disconcerted her, especially when she had the nerve to wink at Wes. Obviously, they were beyond thrilled and relieved when the judge sentenced her to a five-year prison term, but that period passed far too quickly.

Minka was reminded of the conversation, too, while on a case several months ago, not long after she discovered she was expecting Peyton. A newborn and his mother went missing just hours after birth. The woman's husband hadn't made it back in time to witness the amazingly fast at-home birth and was shocked to discover his house empty. After a month-long search, they found the baby with the barren mid-wife, who'd delivered him and taken the two to her parents' house.

The mother was locked in a shed, only released when her baby was hungry.

Truth be known, the case had lurked in the back of Minka's mind ever since. She'd ditched her ideas to give birth at home as soon as she met the distraught father and listened to his terrifying story. More than that, though, she found herself warily scanning her surroundings every time she had a doctor's appointment or shopped for baby clothes. She even refused to show her sonogram to a woman who asked for a peek in the elevator after her first ultrasound.

Now, here she was, pregnant and within reach of a woman who'd expressed interest in her unborn baby once before. Shantelle's presence would be hard to ignore, but Minka had to for the sake of the investigation. The last thing she wanted was to be kicked off the ship— if that were even possible—due to her vengeful spirit. Rather, she'd try to keep her distance but still stay close enough to catch her in any schemes.

Her resolution was soon undermined when the performers lined up to greet the audience as they exited. The four did their best to swerve away from it, but the area was too crowded. All too soon, they stood face-to-face with Shantelle Brayden.

With Shantelle still in her sequenced performance costume, Minka felt like a pauper next to her. "Well, well, well. If it isn't the Avery gang."

Wes was the only one to reply to his former classmate. "Hi, Shantelle. We didn't expect to see you here."

"I never expected to find myself here, either," she agreed in a cold tone. "Guess I have you guys to thank for my career shift."

"Keep telling yourself that," Minka murmured.

"Grumpy, aren't we? I suppose everybody probably is by their seventh year of pregnancy," she taunted.

Minka wanted to jump her, but her husband kept calm. "She's a pro by now. It takes a special lady to carry my kids."

His well-timed remark of admiration won him points with his wife, but Miss Brayden briskly skirted over his kind words. "Well, all the best to you. And by the way, Wes, thanks again for that visit."

They continued on their way, but her last words stuck in Minka's head for the whole jaunt back to the cabins. Even so, she remained silent, not wanting to make a scene and potentially blow their cover. The instant she and Wes retreated into their cabin alone, however, she quizzed him, in no mood for his earlier idea for their evening.

" 'Thanks again for that visit,' " she mocked Shantelle. "What's that supposed to mean? When did you visit her?"

"The day after you did, and believe me, it wasn't a social call or a visit anyone would truly appreciate."

"Why did you go see her?"

Pulling up the desk chair as she sat on the bed, he took her hand. "For the same reason you did. She took as much away from me as she did you. She betrayed me, with no sign of a breach of conscience. So I stormed into her holding cell before you reported to work and balled her out for everything she'd done. I told her I regretted ever knowing her. She didn't say a word."

"She didn't ask to have your son?"

He snickered and shook his head. "The only one I want having my son is you."

She kissed him passionately, but before proceeding any further, she joked, "You aren't telling me we're having a boy, are you?"

Wes grinned. "I don't know. Am I?"

Chapter Six

Minka and Wes slept in later than they had since Caela was born, awaking refreshed the next morning. No one had to rush to get up and make breakfast or get to work, making it easy to linger between the sheets. In that moment, it felt like a true vacation.

But, of course, it wasn't, as the detective reminded herself. Thus, she roused and dressed early enough to dine at the breakfast buffet. Cael met her in the hallway while Wes and Autumn took their time. Claiming a table for two on the top deck, Minka and Cael seized the opportunity to formulate a strategy for their day. With the ship docking at the Bahamian island of Nassau, it posed a dilemma they hadn't discussed. Worried someone would overhear them, Minka confronted him in sign language.

What are we going to do today? She signed the question, inciting a frown of confusion from him. *I mean, we can't keep tabs on the crew while exploring the island, but it'll look suspicious if we all stay behind.*

Seeming more concerned with the croissant he'd been eating, he set the pastry aside to respond, *You tell me. This was your idea.*

None too pleased, she pondered their quandary. *Why don't we take shifts? Two of us can stay on board in the morning while the others enjoy the island. We can switch at lunch. Wes and I will take the morning on the island.*

When we hit Cozumel on Sunday, you guys can have the morning. Sound good?

He nodded in agreement, and after swallowing, he had a suggestion of his own. *Now that we've had a closer look at Logan's fellow performers, we should try to talk with them. Make it casual, like maybe we should put on that we were here before and have fond memories of him.*

She liked the proposition but wanted his input on something she'd been mulling over since running across their former foe. *What if Shantelle outs us as cops? Thankfully, I don't think anyone heard her remarks last night, but she could still confide in somebody in private.*

He took a sip of orange juice, then set it down to free up his hands to stick with ASL. *Just because we're detectives doesn't mean we're working a case at all times. We need vacations as much as the general public.* He changed the subject. *I take it Wes finally admitted to having it out with her.*

You knew?

I was there. I nearly had to cuff him and drag him out of there!

Minka had to smile, envisioning the scene. *Why didn't either of you tell me?*

Because he knew it'd reveal how upset he actually was and that it would make you even angrier. We didn't want add to your stress and endanger your pregnancy with Caela.

Appreciating the sentiment, she was touched by their insight into her state of mind back then. She sat quietly, contemplating the statement, before a sudden jab pierced her stomach. It passed after just a moment, and she rationalized that it was either a digestion pain or maybe even a psychosomatic one from considering the possibility of miscarrying Caela.

Wes and Autumn finally joined them, scooting up another table beside theirs. Minka and Cael related their arrangement for the day just as the ship arrived at the island's port. Eager to explore the same destination they'd enjoyed as newlyweds, Wes downed a quick breakfast before he and Minka set off.

Except for the snorkeling expedition they went on previously, Minka and Wes retraced the same steps they'd taken on their honeymoon. They first visited Fort Fincastle, this time without the assistance of a tour guide, before going to the always-popular straw market. Upon entering the large building, the familiar sights and smells continued to evoke memories. Minka couldn't help but reflect on their first experience on the island...

Still processing the news Dr. Campbell had delivered that morning, Minka couldn't yet face telling her new husband he was about to become a father. They were barely moved into a studio apartment with just enough room for their bed, couch, and a card table in the kitchen area. She had no idea how they'd manage to add a crib, a playpen, a changing table, a swing, and all of the other baby gear.

Just as she was about to hyperventilate with worry, Wes tenderly pointed out a tiny Bahamian baby boy, being cradled by his mother. The loving glimmer in her groom's eyes showed her that she had nothing to fret. When she spotted a booth with personalized straw handbags, she figured out what to do.

He observed her browsing among the names that began with *M* and began to assist her. "You might have to ask them to make a custom one, honey."

"Oh, yes! Here it is." She grasped one hanging just

above her head and displayed it to him; it read, *Mom*. Wes scrutinized it, then his eyes lit up as the realization hit. She nodded, beaming. "It hasn't been seasickness keeping me up at night."

Twelve years later, the same bag hung at the same booth. With hers on her wrist, she held it up to him. "I don't think I have to buy another of these to break the news."

"What news?" he played along.

Shaking her head with a grin, she browsed the vast selection of mostly handmade souvenirs, noting how similar they were to the ones on display twelve years earlier. Even so, she bought a matching purse with Caela's name woven into it. Tempted to get one for Peyton, she glanced Wes's way, who gave her a knowing smile, but opted for the gender-neutral fedora on the opposite wall.

The market seemed more crowded than Minka remembered, though she wondered if that was because she was nearly six months pregnant instead of six weeks. Regardless, she started to feel rather overwhelmed and overheated, and she welcomed a break by the time they reached the exit. Interested in a leather wallet, Wes continued to shop around while she retreated to a nearby bench. Once seated, she released a heavy sigh and caressed her middle, as a little hand or foot fluttered beneath her skin. Finally at peace, she could've easily gone to sleep...that is, if she hadn't noticed Spencer Franklin emerge from the bank across the street.

The cruise director pivoted both ways, his posture rigid, before he strolled down the sidewalk, a thick envelope in his hand. As he tucked it into his back pocket, Minka desperately wanted to follow him, but unarmed and without backup, she had to fight her instincts. Still, she remained focused on his steps, which led in the general direction of the ship, until he vanished from sight.

She cautioned herself not to make a hasty assumption, as there were plenty of reasonable explanations. After all, the cruise was a business, calling for cash for various tasks. There were onboard shops and a casino that could've needed money for the change drawers. On the other hand, it could've been from Franklin's own account. However, that scenario begged the question of why he'd withdraw such a large sum. And why have an offshore account?

So deep in thought, Minka didn't even notice the older lady sitting beside her until she asked, "Is this your first?"

"Excuse me?"

"The baby. Do you have any more children?"

Minka recovered, tapping back into her maternal side. "Oh, yes, we have a seven-year-old daughter."

"She's in for quite a change, then." The woman winked. "Do you know what you're having?"

"My husband and little girl do, but I don't," she told her, chuckling. "It's a long story."

"I've heard it before, believe me. I was a gynecologist for twenty-seven years," she informed her. "You're doing pretty well, it seems?"

"Yes, no problems so far," Minka replied before she remembered the pain that jabbed her earlier that morning.

"That's wonderful. I'm more than happy to help if anything arises while we're out here," the doctor offered, as if reading her mind. "I'm Thelma Plume. I believe we're both on *The Exquisite Marvel?*"

Minka nodded and thanked her, instantly relieved to learn there was help if needed. She considered mentioning the incident, but Wes emerged from the market shortly thereafter, so she wished Thelma a good day. With an hour remaining before they had to head back to the ship to trade places with Cael and Autumn, they strolled to the beach. Though her thoughts had been sidelined from her suspicions about Franklin, they returned to her as she and Wes moseyed along the edge of the brilliant turquoise water. She had so little to raise a brow over, only having beheld him twice now and spoken with him once. Even after that one conversation, something about his manner still didn't sit well with her.

She debated whether or not to address her reservations to Cael when they met on the ship, but she resolved to wait until she had something solid on him to share. For his part, he didn't have much to report from their morning, other than meeting up with two of the stage performers. He'd dropped Logan's name to them like he and Minka planned, but both of Logan's colleagues noncommittedly stated that he didn't work there anymore. The detective did notice sadness in their countenance.

The couples split up, and Minka and Wes returned to the top deck to eat lunch. Having ordered jerk chicken—a local favorite—to-go from an eatery on the island, they chowed down, as Minka reminisced on how much she'd enjoyed the dish on their first visit. Since only a few other passengers remained on-board, the crew members paid them more notice. With the ship providing a meal for any who wanted it, several servers offered her and Wes menus—which they kept declining—until the dessert tray rolled along.

"You can't tell me a pregnant woman isn't in the mood for some sweets!" the middle-aged waitress greeted them.

Tickled by the comment, Minka took an éclair. "I wasn't going to try."

"I only went through it once, but I remember it well. My name's Val, by the way."

"I'm Minka; this is my husband, Wes." After Val offered the father-to-be a dessert, Minka realized she performed in the cabaret show, too. Determined not to let her get away, she spoke up, "We loved your show last night. You have a great voice. Not many people can sing those power ballads, but you sure can."

"I really appreciate that. It's always intimidating, no matter how many times I do it."

Minka reiterated how talented she was before continuing with her plan. "We were here about a year ago and also enjoyed listening to a guy...wasn't his name Logan? When does he perform?"

"Sadly, Logan isn't with us anymore," she stated with somberness. Minka feared she wouldn't get any further than Cael had. To her delight, Val elaborated, "He died suddenly last week. We were all stunned."

They offered their condolences and allowed a somber moment to pass, after which Minka inquired, "Were you two close?"

"Not especially, but I liked him. Everyone did. The one I feel worst for is our director. They were tight."

"Mr. Franklin?" Minka questioned, probably sounding more invested than she should've.

Val nodded. "I'm surprised he didn't take off for the funeral this weekend. I suppose he's trying to keep occupied. We all grieve in different ways, you know?"

They both acknowledged the fact, and Val left them to enjoy their treats. Once she was out of earshot, Wes cornered his wife about her uncharacteristic lack of suave. "And you guys think I can't do undercover work."

"Wes, Franklin acted like he hardly knew Logan when Cael and I talked to him on the phone. In fact, he let on that he was a loner, not that everyone liked him. He didn't seem to be mourning in the least when we told him Logan was dead."

"Maybe they just had a friendly professional relationship, and that's as far as it went. Plus, we all grieve in our own way, like Val said."

She was about to relate observing Franklin at the bank, but another couple sat down in their area. Taking a bite of her éclair, she reasoned it was pointless to argue the matter and waste the fleeting time she had to investigate. She didn't have cause to either accuse or clear Franklin, so she would keep gathering information until she could.

In need of a restroom break after they finished eating, Minka strode to the one on the deck, too desperate to go all the way to the cabin. On her way back, out of the corner of her eye, she caught sight of Spencer Franklin. Though he was just filling out paperwork on the deck, her suspicions arose once again. Given how close he sat, she couldn't resist the urge to engage with him. She couldn't ask about Logan, for fear he'd recognize her voice, but she could get a head start in her investigation of him.

Focused on his forms, he paid no attention to her, until she pulled out the empty chair next to him. "Is it okay if I sit here?"

"Of course. I'm pretty much done, anyway."

"No rush. Frankly, I'm just glad to be out of my cabin."

"It's too nice of a day to be inside. I'm surprised anyone stayed behind."

"Well, my husband and I went out for the morning but didn't want to overdo it. We can't afford to pay for another passenger."

"I see," he said, clearly disinterested. "Well, they're easier to manage in there than out here."

You try it for nine months, buddy.

She grinned, all the while trying to catch a glimpse at his papers. To her disappointment, they appeared to be typical ordering forms for food and beverages, which required his signature. While she learned his middle initial was *J*, she needed more. "So no kids for you?"

Franklin's expression soured, like he bit into spoiled fruit. "Oh, no. My fiancée and I are more than content on our own."

"You're getting married, huh? Have you set a date?"

He shrugged. "Not really. With me here ten months of the year and her in Chicago, a life together isn't easy to picture in the near future. We're hoping everything will fall into place sooner or later."

"I'm sure it will," she replied. "Is Chicago your hometown?"

"No, just hers. We met onboard two years ago. I'm actually from Seattle."

Minka's eyes lit up, as it would help her quest into his life. "How'd you wind up out here?"

"A promotion. I was working on one of our ships over there and was promoted to this position. I preferred our Caribbean route to the Alaskan one," he explained, unwittingly giving her more to use against him.

She supposed the banks were harder to track here, in addition to the warmer weather. "I don't blame you."

Another crewmate approached him, interrupting their chat. "Spence, we have a guest complaining that the fabric of her sheets is affecting her dermatitis."

Franklin rolled his eyes and rose to his feet. "Here we go again. It was nice chatting with you, ma'am. Let us know if there's anything we can do to keep you comfortable—and out of labor."

"Thank you, Mr. Franklin," she offered, eager to learn if he had anything to hide.

****

After her encounter with Franklin, Minka wanted to scout out what she could on the cruise director. She didn't want to nose around the crew, doubting it would accomplish more than putting someone on her trail. Hence, she and Wes exited the ship again in search of free Wi-Fi. The ship charged a daily fee to access the web, and since Wynn claimed the service was spotty, they'd all agreed not to use the amenity unless they had no other choice.

They settled for a sandwich shop near the port, and Minka's quest began with promise due to her knowledge of Franklin's hometown. It quickly waned, however, as his offenses to the law had only been a couple of minor traffic violations. Her visits to his social media pages lent no breakthroughs, either, other than giving her a glimpse into what his fiancée saw in him. Seeming to be quite the bodybuilding fanatic, he was quite chiseled under his polo shirts, and his bride-to-be, in her mini-skirts and bleached blonde hair, appeared to be the vain type.

Stymied, she abandoned the search, and she and

Wes opted to take advantage of being on the grid by calling Caela and his mom, Jaclyn. The usually energetic grandma sounded tired when she answered, and Minka could hear both kids making a ruckus in the background. She couldn't help but grin in amusement. The baby inside her gave a couple good kicks, reminding her she'd soon be in that same predicament.

Both she and Wes talked to Caela about her day and were relieved that she seemed unfazed by their absence. Knowing their next day would be at sea and render them unable to call, they stayed on the phone for as long as she could gab, which amounted to half an hour. While Wes took his turn chatting with her, Minka caught a glimpse of Shantelle Brayden a few tables away, peering at them. She pivoted away when Minka spotted her, but that didn't improve the detective's opinion of her.

On the contrary, Minka sulked over the moment, and it consumed her thoughts for the rest of the day. In fact, she barely remembered to discuss Franklin with Cael. Shantelle's gaze was the only thing she could visualize, and as time progressed, the scene darkened more and more to the point where the dancer became a pirate in the memory.

She wasn't even hungry when dinnertime approached, but because the baby needed nourishment, she conceded. Even so, she was in no mood to sit next to Tula Hawkings and began begging Cael to switch places with her.

"You really think you're going to like being beside Stewart, instead?" he replied. "When he isn't telling stories about his secret work with the feds, he's boring me about the energy crisis and how windmills are going to save the world."

Autumn joined the complaint line, referring to Griffin. "Well, it's better than getting stuck by a foodie who's always expounding on repulsive meat dishes."

"I can tolerate that, if you don't mind Tula," Minka offered, ever the carnivore.

Her sister-in-law complied, so Cael asked Wes, "That means we're swapping, right?"

"No, I like Janine."

Thwarted, Cael shifted to his partner and signed, *Really? This is when you decide to start getting along with my wife?*

Don't get too excited!

He shook his head as she beamed, but her crowing didn't last long. Another jab pierced her middle, similar to the one that morning but slightly more intense. Not wanting to alarm them, she refrained from wincing like she was inclined to and simply rubbed the spot. Given both occurrences struck her right side, she worried it may have been appendicitis, which her brother had dealt with the year before. Just as she began self-diagnosing, her left side took a blow, followed by one to her back.

Noting her unusual movements while they walked, Autumn stepped away from the guys and discreetly inquired, "Are you okay, Minks?"

"I think so. Just having some hunger pains."

"I thought you weren't very hungry."

"I did, too," she admitted. She didn't want to cause any alarm and tried to remain nonchalant. "I've been pretty inactive this afternoon. I probably have to work out some kinks."

Autumn accepted the explanation, but then she introduced another possibility. "Could it be Braxton Hicks contractions?"

Minka doubted it, given hers didn't start until her third trimester with Caela. Just last week, her Lamaze instructor said they could expect them around seven months. Still, she opted to go along with the notion. "Maybe. It's been long enough that I nearly forgot about them."

Their second dinner—mushroom tamales for Autumn and roasted sirloin for everyone else—was more relaxing than their first, as both sisters-in-law better enjoyed their company. The only moment Minka would've changed came when Cael recognized their waiter from the show, and Griffin was talking too loudly for her to listen in on her partner's conversation. It didn't prove to be a big deal, however, with Cael shrugging when she gave him a questioning look.

After they finished their desserts, the group of four departed the dining room and began debating how to spend the rest of their evening. Minka remained in good spirits, having had no pain since before dinner, and playfully suggested they participate in the murder mystery experience. The other three were intrigued by it, particularly Wes, and made their way toward it despite it not set to start for an hour. Located a few doors down the hall from the stage show theater, it shouldn't have surprised Minka to spot Shantelle emerge from the theater and head for what she supposed was the dressing room. Wanting a closer view, she excused herself to use the restroom.

Shantelle already wandered out of sight by the time Minka made it there, but the door stood open and allowed her to peek inside the room's entryway. Nobody occupied it, so she crept into the lounge area. Beside her stood an end table with magazines on it, and her detective's instinct persuaded her to rummage through them. She celebrated a victory when she found an old comic book.

"What are you doing here?" Shantelle's voice shot right through her, making her drop the stack of magazines.

She scrambled to retrieve them, as she desperately clamored for a valid excuse. "I just saw you from a distance and wanted to tell you I didn't like how we left things yesterday."

"I'm sure you didn't. After all, I wasn't being carted off to prison."

It took everything in Minka not to return her disrespect, but in such dire straits, she stayed diplomatic. "I realize we have a messy history, but Wes and I are happy to see you've recovered and are on the right path."

Shantelle sneered. "It's easy for you to call it that. Living in a dream vacation doesn't make for a dream life."

"I understand," Minka stated.

With the unbearable conversation going nowhere, she apologized for bothering her and darted out the door. Hardly as calm as she was feigning, she visited the ladies' room like she'd told her family, sulking the entire way. Her mood worsened when her alleged Braxton Hick flared up again, each pain stinging through her sharper than the last. They didn't stab like the contractions she'd had while delivering Caela, but the intensity rattled her body. She reverted back to her Lamaze exercises, even though they hadn't yet covered them in her current course.

Still, they continued to fire, making her double over in agony. She struggled to make it back out to Wes, Cael, and Autumn, who rushed to her side upon observing her.

"Is everything okay, honey?" her husband cried.

She shook her head and swallowed hard. "I think I'm in labor."

****

Hurrying to the first-aid office and asking for Dr. Plume to be paged, the group tried to keep calm for Minka and Peyton's benefit. Despite her contractions becoming increasingly violent and frequent, the underqualified—and unmotivated—nurses were anything but helpful. They just continued to ask her if she realized twenty-four weeks was the cutoff for cruising. She defended herself, relating that she was at twenty-two weeks, but regret consumed her. She'd be at the mark in nine days, making her argument seem laughable.

Dr. Plume entered the room after Minka begged the staff to summon her over the ship's intercom. As she examined Minka, Wes held her hand and stroked her forehead. His eyes showed his worry, but he kept the mood light. "Maybe Peyton wants to be born on international waters so he or she can have dual citizenship."

She grinned, but her heart sank. She envisioned giving birth on a ship, without the proper care at her disposal. The baby would have to be incubated if he or she had a chance at survival. Even on land, delivering this early would spell a traumatic experience.

Before her imagination could spiral any further, the doctor gave them the report they needed. "You're not dilated at all, and the baby isn't in birthing position. We're not going to welcome another cruiser tonight."

Wes asked the obvious. "Then, why was she in

pain?"

"All I could find was that her blood pressure is elevated. That can typically cause pain and a slight fever, which she also has."

"What can we do about it?" Minka inquired.

"That's the tricky part. Naturally, I can't prescribe anything from here, so all I can suggest is taking it easy for now. You may not even want to leave your cabin, at least for tonight and maybe even tomorrow. Gestational hypertension is nothing to mess with, since it can develop into Preeclampsia. That can be fatal, for mother and baby."

"That really helps lower my blood pressure," Minka mumbled.

In hopes of calming everyone's nerves, Dr. Plume proceeded to stress a balanced diet as well as taking her prenatal vitamins. Minka and Wes thanked the doctor once again for her service, and she assured them she'd check on Minka periodically.

On the way back to the cabin with Cael and Autumn, Wes began his inquisition. "When did you start having symptoms?"

"This morning," she confessed, evoking a scowl of betrayal from him. "But it wasn't anything sustained. Just a momentary jab now and then. Autumn and I thought they were false contractions. Instead of Braxton Hicks contractions, they turned out to be 'Brayden Hicks' contractions."

He didn't crack the slightest smile over her quip. "Regardless of whether the word 'contractions' is preceded by 'false' or whatever, I want to know about it, honey."

"Oh, yeah, I feel my blood pressure dropping by the

minute," she grumbled. "This might not have happened, had it not been for lover girl, Shantelle Brayden."

"Her presence really has you this upset?" Cael asked.

"Of course, it does. We all nearly died at her hand."

"All the more reason not to let her hurt you or the baby this time," Wes stated.

"My point exactly," Minka retorted. "I saw her watching us earlier this afternoon. What if she was plotting? Plus, I ran into her in her dressing room, and she was still acting so hateful."

"Why were you in her dressing room?" Cael dared to ask.

"I followed her when you guys thought I was going to the restroom," she reported with no shame. "And guess what I found there—a vintage comic book."

"You think it's from Logan's collection?" her partner replied.

"I'd say the chances are pretty good. There was only one, though, and it was in a magazine stack."

"If it was stolen, it would take some nerve to display it among his coworkers," Cael said.

Minka acknowledged his point—before another spasm overtook her, and she quivered in pain. Taking control of the situation, Wes ordered her to the cabin, putting an end to the shop talk. Cael and Autumn scurried off to enjoy the rest of the evening.

While the younger couple danced at the salsa club, Minka and Wes lay in bed, watching television and barely speaking. Shantelle had always caused friction between them, and the latest developments didn't help matters along. Of course, Wes detested what she'd done, leading him on a wild goose chase that resulted in him having to enter witness protection. On the other hand, his history with her in high school gave him a soft spot for her that Minka didn't have. Oftentimes, she viewed his leniency of Shantelle as an act of disloyalty.

In an attempt to keep herself distracted from the awkward silence, Minka grasped her tablet. Accepting the Internet usage fee, she researched preeclampsia. Her findings revealed she didn't have many of the risk factors for it, which relieved her because the horror stories were a dime a dozen. Some women miscarried, as others were on bed rest for months, nearly bleeding to death. Her fears worsened when another round of spasms grabbed her and also when she noticed her swelling hands, another symptom of the condition.

Just in the nick of time, Dr. Plume stopped in to check on her patient before her own bedtime. Wes gave his wife some privacy, although the doctor merely checked both mother and baby's heartbeat as well as Minka's blood pressure with a stethoscope. She informed her that it'd dropped in the past two hours, though the expectant mother could only wonder how.

"We're still not in the clear yet," Dr. Plume cautioned. "But if you keep doing what you're doing, you'll probably be able to do a little more tomorrow."

Minka nodded with a smile and wanted to let her go on her way, but she had to ask one question. "Should I be worried if I have any more pain?"

"Have you had any recently?"

"About ten minutes ago."

The doctor hesitated but reported it wasn't unusual to experience spasms with her blood pressure still a bit elevated. That said, she wanted Minka to call her if they intensified or became more frequent. As she left, Minka asked if her swelling hands signaled anything.

"You're pregnant; you'll be fortunate if your nose is normal sized by the time you give birth!"

Despite being suddenly self-conscious about her nose, Minka laughed in relief. After the door closed, she retrieved her tablet and exited the article about preeclampsia. She had the tendency to become overwhelmed by the worst-case scenarios, especially when it concerned her kids. Unless absolutely necessary, she shied away from such studies and instructed her curious mind that she needed to do so now, at a time when she was supposed to avoid stress.

Upon clearing out the opened apps on the screen, Minka's eyes were captivated by her wallpaper, recently changed to her latest sonogram. True, she'd been through it all before, but she still marveled at each ultrasound as much as the last, unable to believe there was a little person who depended solely on her. The concept both invigorated and scared her, always reminding her of the weighty responsibility she carried. That in mind, she was coerced into resolving the matter at hand, aware that her choice to continue living in anger may well rob her of that precious child. Thus, when Wes rejoined her on the bed, she took the initiative to make peace.

"I'm sorry I let it get this far," she offered. When he said nothing, she added, "You know how I feel about her."

"Everyone knows how you feel about her, Minka. Even our seven-year-old," he replied, given she'd told Caela several bedtime stories, in which Shantelle played the evil villain.

"And once again, I'm the one in the wrong."

"No, you're not. I just wish you'd understand how

little she actually has over you." He shifted onto his side, locking gazes with her. "The month I spent in WITSEC—it's long gone without any lasting consequences. That day she and DeSoto almost killed us was the day we were reunited, and it's basically why we're here now. For her part, she's miserable in her life and doesn't pose a true threat to us...other than upsetting you to the point of losing our child."

"I never thought of it that way," she admitted.

He caressed her cheek. "I would've been completely content if she'd never entered our life and messed it up like she did, but to some extent, it led us here. There's nowhere else I'd rather be."

"Me, neither." Minka kissed him, before joking, "One of us may need to sleep on the couch tonight to avoid doing something that might elevate my blood pressure!"

Grinning, he leapt from the bed and grabbed his pillow. "Parenthood!"

Chapter Seven

After an uneventful night, Minka was eager to get up and move around as normal, without a trace of the pain she experienced the day before. Her husband, however, hesitated and suggested she lay low until Dr. Plume checked in on them. As she'd promised, the doctor arrived on her way to breakfast, and to Minka's chagrin, she suggested she still take it easy for the morning.

"We'll just be at sea all day, so it isn't like you'll be missing much," she told her, having no clue of their ulterior motives for being aboard. "The ocean will still be there this afternoon, barring a phenomenon."

Minka chuckled and thanked her, trying to hide her disappointment. Wes offered to stay with her, but considering his love of the sea, she declined and told him the television would keep her company. After choosing a cooking show, it didn't take her long to reach for the phone and order room service.

Twenty minutes later, Val knocked on the door with Minka's omelet and orange juice.

"Well, hello again," the cheerful woman greeted, wheeling in the cart. "I just saw your hubby upstairs and wondered where you were. The little one give you a rough night?"

"Sort of. I guess we overdid it yesterday, so I'm trying to rest up a bit. Wes was willing to stick with me, but he enjoys the water so much that I couldn't deny him that."

"You have the opposite problem I do; mine's terrified of it! He's such a coward that he won't set foot on this ship even while we're docked to bring me something I forgot at home. Thank goodness I'm only part-time. We'd never see each other." She smirked. "Then again, after thirty years together…"

The ladies shared a laugh before Val continued on her route. Minka scarfed down her breakfast efficiently, having eaten no snacks after last night's dinner. Thus, she had no trouble cleaning her plate before the kitchen staff returned to collect her dishes, but she wasn't prepared for who they sent.

"Are you finished with your meal, ma'am?" he asked upon entering.

"Yes, thank you," she replied, only then recognizing Logan's roommate, Wynn McCallum. She instantly recoiled, almost ducking under the sheets so he wouldn't get a good look at her. Her voice gave her away, though.

"Aren't you the detective who was here last week to investigate Logan's death?"

She could've tried to lie, but with a deaf accent and a pregnant belly, it would've only added to his suspicion. "I am. It's good to see you again. After our visit, I realized how beautiful this was, and my husband and I were in the market for a babymoon, so here we are."

"I see."

His somber reply shamed her, as she appreciated how shallow the story surely appeared to him. His friend was killed nine days earlier, and an investigator who was supposed to be looking for the responsible party had just decided to take the week off—at his place of employment, no less.

"That's what I'm supposed to tell you, anyhow." Motioning for him to close the door, she rebelled against her and Cael's agreement. "The truth is my partner and I really feel something on-board led to his murder, and we're here to try to determine what that was. But nobody can know, in case someone involved hears and covers his or her tracks."

"I'll be silent, I promise. I want justice for Logan more than anyone," he vowed. "If I can help at all, don't hesitate to ask."

She did hesitate, worried she'd already confided too much in him. If he played any part in his roommate's demise or knew who had, she could've just blown their entire mission in that one moment. Even so, there was a question they should've asked a week ago, and risky or not, she couldn't let her chance slip again.

"After you left us in your cabin, we never found the comic books you mentioned he had. Any idea where they could be?"

"No, he always stored them under his bed. He read one on his last voyage."

She wondered about the one in the performers' lounge but didn't want to admit it. "Did he take it to rehearsal, maybe?"

Wynn snickered. "No, he kept one of his spares there at all times."

His statement deflated her high hopes about her discovery the previous day, but it also solidified the fact the collection was, indeed, missing. Of all people, Wynn should've understood if and why Logan would've relocated his prized possessions. The fact that he didn't only reinforced her suspicion of it being taken without

Logan's consent. Now, she just had to decide whether or not to inform her partner of the interesting conversation.

Still trapped in her cabin, however, the prospect seemed like days away. To pass the time, she grabbed her tablet. Tied in with the Wi-Fi for twelve more hours, she emailed Gus Channing with the latest updates, leaving out the run-in with Wynn. While she was at it, she also checked in with Sadie, in hopes she'd check her inbox after Lamaze class. Although everything took a little longer to load than it did at home, she deemed the service satisfactory for the tasks she had to perform.

Dr. Plume returned earlier than Minka expected, and this time, she gave her the thumbs-up to rejoin civilization. Wes entered within seconds after she headed out, indicating that he'd been waiting outside, and his romantic side reawakened during her brief absence.

"What's this?" she wondered of the envelope in his hand.

"Your push present."

"I hope not to be pushing for at least four months," she joked. When she opened the envelope, she couldn't believe her eyes. "A couple's massage? You've vowed never to even enter a spa."

"Dr. Plume said it'd be good for you and the baby," he explained. "Plus, you'll have to take a break from your spying for at least an hour."

Her shoulders suddenly tensed. "We're doing it here? Now? I thought we'd wait a couple of…months."

"We'll be off the ship by then. Plus, what good would it do the baby?"

"It would relax his or her exhausted mother," she replied, but he still didn't catch on. "Besides, I may be a few pounds lighter."

His wife's insecurities finally dawned on him, and he assured her, "Honey, you're more beautiful than ever when you're pregnant. I tell you that every day."

"Sure, to you, I am, but not to a twenty-five-year-old, size-zero masseuse who's never seen a stretch mark in her life!"

"I told them about you, and they said they work with babymooners all the time." He took her by the hand. "Just trust me."

Yet again, the twinkle in his eyes and coy smile made her buy into his charm. That said, she still insisted on changing into a tank top and shorts, in hopes of not being asked to disrobe any further. Her plan worked, as her masseuse, who was a bit older than she anticipated, told her she could do whatever made her comfortable.

It wasn't the conventional couple's treatment for a number of reasons. Instead of being side-by-side, Wes was instructed to lie on the table, while Minka, who was unable to lie on her stomach, straddled a massage bench. Nonetheless, she thoroughly enjoyed her back massage and began to wonder why she hadn't indulged in such pampering sooner. Before long, though, she realized the answer.

"Sorry!" her husband excused himself, chuckling, as his digestive system proclaimed itself.

On the opposite side of the room with her face between cushions, Minka soon smelled the stench that followed. Just when she reckoned she couldn't be more embarrassed, it happened a second, third, and fourth time. For his part, Wes lost all shame, with each occurrence making him laugh harder and harder. His German masseuse—who didn't speak a lick of English—started to giggle, as well, and her colleague eventually did, too. The only one who failed to find the humor in it was his mortified wife.

She kept quiet, however, until her masseuse told her to lie down on her back on the table beside him. He flipped over at the same time, and she whispered in his ear, demanding he go to the restroom. He obliged, leaving her alone with her masseuse. An American woman, she began rubbing her client's swollen middle, doing her best to ease her tension.

As she gently kneaded her hands all around the bump, the baby inside reacted well. "You have a couple of active ones in there."

"There's just the one, that I'm aware of, at least," Minka corrected her.

The woman acted ashamed of her mistake. "Oh, I'm so sorry. My next appointment must be the one expecting twins."

Minka told her not to worry, since she'd noticed how many others were cruising for two—or three. In the awkward silence that followed, she conjured up a way the woman could make it up to her, even without realizing it.

"So are you acquainted with the rest of the staff well?"

"Some of them." She shrugged. "I mainly know the ones who come in here or who go on breaks at the same time I do."

"I'll bet the stage performers frequent you guys, with the workout they get every show."

"Yes, the majority books an appointment at least once a week," she said, delighting Minka.

She paused, calculating her next move but ultimately just dove in. "We really enjoyed the show. I loved the movie soundtrack medley. The brunette singer who did most of the female leads was great."

"Yeah, that's Shantelle. We're good friends. She's so sweet. You'd never figure how much she's been through."

Minka had to try. "Like what?"

She hesitated but not for long. "Well, she had a broken engagement a few years back, which upended her life. This wasn't her pick of a career, but she wanted a fresh start. Just when she finally began to embrace it and found a new guy, he died."

Shocked by that little bomb, Minka became desperate to verify if this lover was Logan Baris, but she'd have to be subtle. "That's horrible. Did he work here on the ship, too?"

"Yes, he was also a singer. He sang a lot of the duets with her, in fact. I'm amazed she can still perform them."

Minka could only hope her interest wouldn't cause alarm. "How long were they together?"

"A few months. They kept it quiet for a while, but word started getting around right before he died. They may not have been together for long, but she was crazy for him. I'd never seen her so happy."

Minka offered a somber groan and wondered what else she could get her to divulge, but Wes returned, putting an end to her sleuthing. Inside, she had to grin over defying his earlier statement about halting her investigation, but she wouldn't crow. He'd be livid to learn that she was again dwelling on Shantelle when he meant for her to relax.

With their massage session drawing to a close, she contemplated how she should handle her discovery. It was, indeed, a bombshell, for it thrust Shantelle deeper into the crosshairs of the case than they already surmised. Considering she was engaged to a criminal the last time they dealt with her, Minka didn't deem it a stretch to imagine her going after another bad boy or converting him into one.

Thus, Minka couldn't keep this from Cael, even at the expense of his cynical tongue. She was merely doing her job, she told herself, and just as she would at the precinct, she was focusing on someone with priors. She didn't wish for Shantelle to be involved in Logan's murder. Instead, she sympathized with the dancer for losing another love so tragically.

But her partner didn't regard it that way when she related her breakthrough over lunch.

He snickered, eating his meal while Wes and Autumn retrieved theirs. "You just can't quit, can you?"

"This is not about our history," she insisted. His pointed scowl at her needled her conscience. "Well, not altogether."

Cael snorted. "There's my Minks."

"You can't honestly say this is minor, though. She might not be a suspect yet, but she's an asset, for sure. We need to learn what she knows."

"And how, do you propose, do we do that? Sneak into her dressing room again? It worked out so well yesterday for you."

"Cael!"

He put a soothing hand on her shoulder and gave her a moment to calm down before he rationally explained his concerns. "Jokes aside, this is going to be a challenge. She knows we're detectives, and she'd most likely be aware that we weren't on this ship last year, like we've been claiming to everyone else. She'd catch on to us, and if she does have something to hide, it wouldn't be good. We have three days to get anywhere with this, so we can't slip up."

She agreed with his reasoning, but the realization of their fragile position discouraged her. It seemed like this would be as far as they went, the unexpected brick wall dropped in the middle of their game. Even worse, she believed she could almost touch the grand finale, but the touchy circumstances would prevent her from getting any closer.

Immersed in her thoughts, Minka nearly jumped when Autumn, upon returning to her seat, reached over to touch her bump. "Someone's getting a good workout."

"Tell me about it." Minka shifted gears, from detective to mommy. "It's a good sign, according to Dr. Plume. She says babies slow down in activity just before birth, so as long as this one's moving, we don't have to worry."

"Tyson went bonkers when I was in labor," Autumn disagreed. "Come to think of it, I guess that was Cael!"

"Hey!" Her husband playfully threw a straw wrapper at her.

The couples enjoyed the jovial moment, exchanging several delivery room anecdotes. They were just finishing their lunch when Minka noticed Spencer Franklin at the same table she'd spotted him the day before, this time accompanied by two other crew members. While she assessed him, she still couldn't suppress her instincts that he somehow had a hand in Logan's death. Then again, she assumed Shantelle did, too, so maybe she was zeroing in on the ones she was most familiar with and disliked.

Reproving herself, Minka resolved to keep her mind

and eyes as open as she had when they boarded. That alleviated her thoughts for a moment until she became overwhelmed again by the task. There were still so many workers they had yet to meet face-to-face, let alone engage in conversation. With how busy they were and the fact that the detectives couldn't announce their presence, the chances of them catching a lead—that didn't involve Franklin or Shantelle—seemed to be shrinking.

The wave of disappointment started to return, followed by the lingering question of if they'd be closer to solving the case had they stayed home. That in mind, Minka, having brought her tablet to the table, checked her email again but received no reply from Sadie. Gus had responded, only to acknowledge her update and counsel her to stay away from Shantelle. Used to the warning by now, she grimaced and deleted it.

Remembering their determination when they booked the trip, she took a deep breath and strived to have a relaxing time, if nothing else. Sure, she'd continue to remain alert to anyone who may have more to offer on Logan, but she also needed to embrace the beautiful experience, instead of sulking over a lack of leads. The guys unwittingly helped that along, surprising her and Autumn with hair and makeup appointments in the salon to prepare for Captain's Night, the most formal evening of the week.

Venturing back to the salon where Wes and Minka had their massage, the ladies found it much more crowded than earlier. Everyone clearly had the same idea to indulge in some beauty time for the elegant occasion, and the room buzzed with talk about dresses and nail tips. Since Minka never had a real girlfriend growing up with whom she chatted over such topics, she sank down into her seat a bit, unaccustomed to the atmosphere. Nonetheless, she tried to make the most out of it. In the end, it proved worthwhile, with both of them feeling more beautiful than they had since their wedding days.

To keep the mood special, they entreated the guys to get dressed in one cabin and they in the other, not even catching a glimpse of them before they were in their gowns. Their husbands acquiesced, albeit somewhat begrudgingly, comparing it to a corny prom.

"Your dad's going to kill me if I get you pregnant," Wes taunted his wife when he handed over her dress with his eyes shut. "Oh, yeah, I already did!"

Rolling her eyes, she entered Cael and Autumn's cabin, as she told her sister-in-law, "Don't forget your birth control. The guys are scared they'll get in trouble if we end up pregnant. It's too late for me, of course."

Autumn sighed. "I wish that were a problem."

"What do you mean?"

She paused before answering, "I may not be able to conceive again."

"Huh? Why not? You're an expert on fertility. You had me doing all kinds of tricks to get pregnant," Minka reminded her, not adding the fact that none of them worked.

"Well, knowledge isn't everything, Minka." She plopped down onto the bed. "I saw my doctor a few weeks ago for a prenatal exam. Cael and I want to start trying within the year, so I wanted to ensure I was well enough. It initially appeared that I'm in good shape, but the ultrasound they did on my uterus showed several medium-sized polyps."

Tears began to form in her eyes, and Minka joined

her on the bed to offer her a hug, lost for words. It was news she'd expect from anyone else, even herself, before she would Autumn. Since she'd met her, she'd been the essence of health and committed to doing the best thing for her body...sometimes to the point of annoyance. Needless to say, this was definitive proof that calamity didn't discriminate.

Regaining her composure, Autumn continued, "The doctor said they're probably benign, but it's doubtful I could conceive if we tried, which he warned us not to for now. I'm having them removed next week, and they'll do a biopsy to test if it's..."

Understanding why she couldn't bear to say the word, Minka sought to comfort her. "I'm sure it isn't."

Autumn nodded in appreciation and drifted away from her. "Anyhow, we've kept it quiet, not wanting to take away yours and Wes's joy, but I guess that's why I've been a bit pushy about your learning the gender and all. This could be our last baby for a long time, and I want to be part of it."

Minka clutched her hand and allowed her to feel Peyton's kicks. "I want you to be, too."

"Hey, little one. I'm your auntie," she murmured.

Drawn closer to her sister-in-law than ever before, Minka told her with sincerity, "I can't wait until you make me one again, too."

****

Recovering from the serious conversation, Minka and Autumn relished in getting ready for dinner. The men, as always, finished well before them and were waiting at the door, taking turns complaining. It didn't make their wives rush in the least but arguably had the opposite effect. When they emerged, however, with

Minka in a wine-colored empire dress and Autumn donning a strapless silver gown, the protests fell silent…at least on the gentlemen's part.

"What are you wearing?" Autumn questioned her husband.

"The suit I wore at our wedding, which you chose," he remarked of the tailed tuxedo.

"But I did not pick out the cowboy hat or those boots."

"And I still can't see why. Why have a tux with coattails without going for a Wild West theme?"

Minka was struggling to suppress her hysteria, until her eyes slid to Wes, and she had to question, "Okay, big brother, what's up your sleeve?"

"Nice word choice, honey." He slid up his sleeve to reveal a hook substituting his left hand. He followed it up by taking an eye patch out of his pocket and putting it on his head, as he spoke in a pirate's voice, "It is Captain's Night, me lady!"

Minka threw up her hands. "Oh, geez!"

"I was going to put on my dreads, but I was afraid of pushing you into labor. If you feel all right, though—"

Pretending, his wife made a jarring movement and grabbed her stomach. "Better not chance it, babe."

The other three shook their heads and started on their trek to the dining room. Unlike the previous two nights, there was an area off to the side for photos, complete with a backdrop and all, where a line had already formed. It only encouraged Wes and Cael's cracks about the prom-like scene, making the women question if their photos would be worth all of the embarrassment. Given that it wasn't a common occasion for any of them, however, they decided to suffer through the humiliation.

To top it off, Wes and Minka took their place in line just in time to have Tula and Stewart wander up behind them. With Mrs. Hawkings in a princess-style ball gown covered in sequins, Minka wondered if the camera would capture anything but refracted light.

"I see someone's feeling better." Tula embraced Minka and bent down to address the mother-to-be's belly. "You had us all very worried, sweet Peyton."

Minka lifted her brow at Wes, displeased the stranger was privy to both her scare and their child's name.

Her husband informed her, "I forgot to mention we had breakfast together."

She was certain he hadn't merely forgotten, but she stayed silent and allowed Tula to elaborate. "Yes, it was lovely. I learned so much about you two. Your husband's been through a lot, being orphaned and kidnapped. I really hope you find his birth family tomorrow."

"I'm confident they'll turn up someday," Minka replied between gritted teeth.

"They'd be thrilled to see he met a wonderful girl like you and has two babies of his own."

She proceeded to reveal that Wes had shared their love story—which, thankfully, proved to be the truth, with a few minor exaggerations—and then imparted her own tale. By the time she finished relating how she fell for Stewart when he changed her car's air filter, Minka had subtly switched off her cochlear. Wes startled her when he took her hand to lead her to the photography platform.

The same photographer who'd snapped a shot of

them after their first dinner was manning the camera and seemed to have a well-trained eye for staging the scene. Even helping Minka arrange her dress's short train, he directed Wes to place a hand on her baby bump, but he winced upon noting her husband's fake hook. Blushing, Minka could only imagine what he and the others in line were thinking, including Tula, who was under the impression that he'd been raised by pirates.

Off to the side, Autumn asked to have a photo taken with them after their solo one, and despite the line, the shutterbug obliged. As he instructed her and Cael on where to stand, Minka paid more notice to the man's appearance and suddenly recognized him from Franklin's social media pages. A moment later, she realized he also shared the director's table that afternoon. Neither fact implicated him—or Franklin, for that matter—in Logan's murder, but she still deemed it valuable information to her study of the man in charge.

They moved along once the pictures were taken, and although early for dinner, they took their spots at their table. Griffin and Janine Garets, who'd also posed for a portrait, were already seated, as well, and the former detective had managed to swipe a sampling from the unsupervised dessert cart.

"Some cop he is, huh?" Janine teased when they sat down.

"I never took an oath to serve and protect food," he replied, clearly savoring his caramel-layered parfait.

His wife crossed her arms. "Well, you could at least share."

"You wouldn't like it; it's too sweet."

The younger couples reveled in the exchange, with Minka wishing the Garets would move to central

Florida for their retirement. Nonetheless, her mind revolved back to the case. Considering she sat next to a seasoned detective with many more years of experience, it was tempting to consult with him about it. She knew her partner wasn't keen on the idea, but when he strolled away from the table to go to the restroom, she took advantage of the moment.

Trying to keep her query general, she asked, "During your years in Narcotics, what were the hallmarks of a case that involved the drug industry?"

"Pretty much what you'd expect—the typical names popping up, suspicious banking activity, unexpected deaths. We always tried to stay ahead of them, but they eventually found a way to surprise us. I can't say it never bothered me. I enjoyed my job, but it frustrated me after a while, like trying to catch dust particles in the air."

She nodded, fully able to relate. "I think we all feel that way at some point."

"I just had to keep telling myself we may not save everybody, but whoever we can still matters. It's someone's spouse, parent, sibling, or child."

Minka appreciated the sentiment, having drilled the same thought into her head during times of disappointment. She wanted to continue the discussion, but she struggled to keep it vague. Just when she began to formulate a plan, Cael returned to his seat. Griffin's observations swirled around in her brain, as the indicators he mentioned were all at play in Logan's murder. True, their investigation into Thiago Fontanilla had proven fruitless, but that didn't mean Logan Baris wasn't colluding with another dealer.

Reminding herself not to be narrow-minded, however, she enjoyed her dinner while always keeping a watchful eye on the staff. All said and done, nothing but the delicious Japanese-themed meal beckoned her attention. She did her best to block out Tula and Autumn's forty-minute debate about rice cookers. After they finished, they once again deliberated over how to occupy the rest of their evening. Wes suggested they follow through with their plans from the night before of going to the murder mystery show.

"You just can't get enough of playing detective, can you?" his wife teased.

He winked. "That must be why we're such a good match."

After she accepted his checkmate, Cael added, "Speaking of which, stay away from the stage show theater this time, Minks."

She vowed to comply, but in an attempt not to repeat history, they opted to go to another floor entirely until their activity was scheduled to start. Having not yet explored the variety of shops, Minka and Autumn jumped at the chance to do so, prompting the brothers to indulge in their childlike thirst for the nearby arcade.

Heading into the largest—and most affordable—gift shop, the ladies browsed the vast array of souvenirs and consulted each other over what to buy for their family members. They both selected several items for themselves as well as their friends and family and before long needed a cart. With her hands less full, Minka strode over to retrieve one, and while she unloaded her selections into it, Shantelle Brayden approached her.

"Hello, detective." Noticeably more meek, her next words shocked Minka more than the first. "I noticed you in here and wanted to…apologize for my behavior yesterday. I ran into Cael this morning, and he mentioned your close call with the baby. I never meant to upset you to that degree."

Numerous responses spun through her mind—none of them kind—but in the spirit of mending fences, Minka replied, "I appreciate that."

Seeming to be perplexed by how to proceed, Shantelle shuffled her feet. "I never expected to face any of you again, and it's been even harder than I could've imagined. You're all reminders of my battles, and I just really didn't need that right now. I'm not blaming you for that, though. It's merely the way things worked out."

"I understand," Minka offered, sure she wasn't a fond memory of anyone she'd helped to arrest and convict.

She expected the dancer to trot away, but Shantelle surprised her by elaborating, "You see, I was starting to feel like my life was finally on the upswing, but my reason for feeling that way is gone now." She handed Minka her phone, which displayed Logan's picture. "His name's Logan Baris. He was murdered in Orlando last week, and I wondered if it's your department investigating it?"

Unable to believe the conversation was taking this turn, Minka had to think quickly. Given that she wasn't apprised of her and Cael's recent promotion, she said, "I can check with the detectives in Homicide."

"That means a lot to me," Shantelle replied, her voice cracking. She slipped a piece of paper out of her pocket. "If you do track down the investigators, I'd like you to pass on this note to them."

Taking it, Minka unfolded it and recognized Logan's handwriting from his driver's license. It read:

I can't stick around here anymore, baby. I take no

*pride in what I'm doing, and I can't keep it up. I promise
to come back for you when I'm the man you deserve.*

All My Love,

Logan

"He gave this to you shortly before he died?"

Shantelle nodded. "I found it in my cabin when I
boarded for the next voyage. After we docked, we both
headed home for some fresh clothes; I didn't even kiss
him goodbye. A day later, he was killed."

"What did you initially make of his note?"

"I had no idea what to think. We both had our
moments of discontent over our careers. He was way too
talented to remain a cabaret singer and had been offered
several auditions from hot-shot guests. I wondered if
he'd pursued an opportunity like that, but I couldn't
understand why he wouldn't tell me that in advance. I
would've happily joined him."

Countless other questions circled Minka's mind, but
in an effort to keep her façade intact, she simply assured
her, "I'll make sure this gets into the right hands."

Chapter Eight

Shantelle wanted their help as much as they wanted hers.

The idea bewildered Minka as she attempted to shop and not crack around Autumn, who, thankfully, hadn't observed them chatting. Tucking Logan's note into her purse, she cringed when she envisioned informing Cael of the development after his implicit orders to steer clear of the dancer. Then again, Shantelle had approached her, not the other way around.

Remembering that he, too, had a conversation with her and didn't share it with his partner, Minka didn't sweat staying silent for a while. Besides, they were supposed to focus on another mystery that evening— albeit a fictitious one. Once she and Autumn finished their mini shopping spree, they met their husbands in the concourse and took their bags to the cabins. Ready for their night of investigating, they returned to the banquet hall where it took place, finding themselves transported to a rehearsal dinner for 'Traci and Levi'.

"Welcome!" the supposed bride-to-be exclaimed. "Thank you for coming to our big night before our big day!"

Minka could only hope her overwhelming bubbliness was part of the act, and Wes seemed to echo her thoughts when he murmured, "I'm beginning to rethink this."

Nonetheless, the four of them greeted her and played along by expressing their congratulations. Autumn even proceeded to ask for a glimpse of her ring, a cheap fake like the kind Caela was always gazing at in the ten-dollar carousel at the bargain stores. After exchanging pleasantries, Traci handed them an envelope with their characters' names and backstories inside. She instructed them to take a seat wherever they liked and to open them there.

Unfolding her character description, Minka had to laugh, reciting " 'Willa Baxter, Traci's alcoholic cousin.' That doesn't compliment the pregnant belly very well."

"It's okay, babe. I, Dexter Bradford, have a Ph.D. and my own psychiatric practice. I helped your cousin overcome her eating disorder and can help you sober up."

The four chuckled, and Cael and Autumn related that their characters were both former classmates of Levi's, with him working as an accountant while she managed a bakery. Ironically, Griffin and Janine soon arrived, making for three trained professionals at the table. It was clear, however, that Detective Garrets mainly cared about the refreshments instead of solving the crime.

After the attendees had filed in, the rehearsal dinner began with a speech from the father-of-the-bride, followed by ones from the bride and groom. During the groom's love-infused ode to his future wife, he started to grapple with a cough, which became increasingly violent as his discourse continued. Before long, he couldn't speak, until he fell onto the table and expired.

With their mouths agape, the wedding party cried

out and fled the room, leaving their guests to identify the culprit among them. While the cast took an intermission, those present were encouraged to mingle and get acquainted with the others around them, much like the Averys had already done. It called for impromptu acting, which about half the group seemed to welcome, whereas the others hesitated, including Griffin.

As he munched on his cake, Janine tried to rally him into the spirit of the game. "Come on, honey. How can anyone solve this without the whole pool of suspects? You should be able to relate."

He played off his reluctance to participate. "I sure can, and I know the majority of suspects aren't willing to parade around, sharing their life stories."

"Might that explain your reluctance?" his wife replied.

Griffin took another bite and lifted an eyebrow. "Do you really think I'd admit it if it did?"

His wife gave way to her distinct cackle, a sound the Avery clan had grown accustomed to by now. The other two detectives weren't overly enthused about the activity, either, as Cael had never been the actor type, and Minka finally found a comfortable position in her straight chair. Taking a cue from Janine, their spouses joked that their opposition may be a declaration of guilt.

"I bet Levi's champagne was poisoned," Wes theorized aloud. "Sounds like something a lush would do!"

Minka answered his accusation with an eye roll, and Autumn chimed in about Cael's alter ego. " 'Wallace' over here has always been jealous of him. Levi was better at him in everything, making the varsity football team three years before he even made it off the bench."

"Where are you getting this?" Cael demanded.

"Two semesters of drama in high school," she told him.

Impressed, Minka smiled across at them, before her mind began to drift back to their real murder mystery. She wondered if Sadie emailed her back yet. She glanced at the clock above their table, and from their conversations in recent weeks, she figured she was already in her pajamas. Like her, Sadie had noticed a significant decrease in energy as her second trimester progressed.

She continued to contemplate their last conversation, even as fellow guests approached their table to learn their backgrounds. While she relented and gave a monologue of her struggles with scotch, she suddenly made a connection she never could've expected. All at once, she recalled Sadie's report about the poor condition of Logan's lungs, calling to mind the visual of Levi suffering a cough in his final moments. Being a common cause of death in setups like this, it could've been a coincidence, but still, Minka couldn't dismiss her shocking notion…

What if Logan's killer took cues from the show?

If the theory in itself didn't alarm her enough, the bride reappeared and shook Minka with the announcement, "I found a note!"

Now invested in the scene, Minka straightened up in her seat, hanging onto every syllable.

" 'My Dearest Traci,' " the actress began. " 'I can't keep loving you in secret. I've tried to tell you my feelings time and again, but I realize this is my final chance. You'd think I'd be better at expressing myself, but I guess I've always left that to you. In silence, I've fallen in love with you, and I know you better than anyone. Levi isn't the one for you, and this is all I could think of to do to show you that. Please, forgive me.' "

Minka retracted a bit, disappointed that this note hardly mirrored Logan's, but she remained hopeful that a link to the case might arise. Thus, she rose to her feet and related, "I think I'll snoop around, after all."

Wes stood up, too. "They baited you, huh?"

"I'm getting stiff." She shrugged, not wanting to reveal her true motive. To sell her story, she stretched her back, until realizing she still wore her formal gown, which could've easily given way if she tested it. She hadn't planned to indulge in desserts as much as she had when she picked it out five days—and a couple of pounds—earlier.

Joined by Cael and Autumn, they strolled around the room and mingled with the other willing participants. The cast returned to the room, fielding inquiries about the tragedy. Enough people had entered the competition that there was a crowd circling each of them, making it hard to get within hearing—or even lip-reading—range. Nobody took much interest in the note from the killer, laying out for examination, so the detectives and their spouses took advantage of the vacancy.

Minka wasn't afraid to grab it first, recounting the words Traci had read aloud. Penned in a unique purple color, the remarks about the writer's expressing himself and his silence gave her a theory, but she suppressed it, deeming the possibility as just too simple. Handing it over to Wes and Cael, she no sooner caught a peek of the other side of the paper and recaptured it.

"Is she this possessive at work?" Wes asked his brother.

"On her good days," Cael muttered under his breath.

Ignoring them, she flipped over the note to find faded ink, but it was clearly a receipt. Placing it under a nearby lamp, she leaned in close to try to make out what it said, certain it was supposed to be discovered. She peered at the line where the only purchase was listed and could decipher enough of the letters to understand what it uncovered.

"The killer bought a toaster oven off of their registry," Minka announced.

Before any of them could question her further on it, she scurried to the gift table, having already wondered why there'd be one at a rehearsal. She began to unwrap packages in no time, making quite a spectacle. None of the cast made any objections, however. In the center of the group, she located the infamous toaster and removed the attached card. When she read the name, she couldn't believe her instincts had been correct.

"Do you have something to share, ma'am?" the head waiter questioned her.

"Yes, I know who killed Levi," Minka declared, triggering a canned gasp from the actors. Embracing the role, she made her definitive accusation. "This note was carelessly written on the back of a receipt for this toaster. The enclosed card, in purple handwriting that matches the note to Traci, identifies the giver—and killer—as Dr. Dexter Bradford!"

When she pointed to Wes, all eyes shifted to him.

Ever the showman, he disputed her claim. "She's a drunk; she doesn't even know where she is right now."

"It doesn't take a completely sober person to see how you feel about her." His wife played along and stumbled against a chair, inciting a collective chuckle from the audience. "I'll bet you fell for Traci 'in silence' while she poured her heart out to you in therapy. That's why you should be better at expressing yourself, Mr. Ph.D."

At last, the bride spoke up, "You've always told me how beautiful I was, and I just assumed you were trying to build my confidence."

More incriminating reports were fired against the psychiatrist, including the father-of-the-bride's report of witnessing him emerge from the kitchen with a pill bottle. Recovered by the maid-of-honor, the bottle contained a seizure medication with a side effect of causing hyperventilation. With that, security guards arrested 'Dexter' and momentarily escorted him outside.

The guests were invited to stay as long as they wished, and Minka and Wes posed for a picture with the cast. They then retreated to their table, with Minka being greeted by Griffin's signature "Check you out," before the four decided to escape the stuffy room.

She consulted the clock on their way out and realized she had another forty-five minutes before her day of Internet access elapsed. She made plans to meet her family at the table where they ate breakfast the previous morning and scurried to her cabin. After using the bathroom, she collected her tablet and checked her email, which contained nothing from Sadie. Being a Saturday, she figured she shouldn't have even bothered the busy woman.

Just the same, she took the device with her in case she received something in the next half-hour or if one of the others wanted to access the web. After she reunited with them, the four stayed on the lower deck for a change and ambled up to the banister to gaze over the sea.

"I'm not sure we should be this close to the edge with a murderer in our midst," Minka joked. "To think, the father of my children…"

"I think him being a shrink is scarier than him being a killer," Cael added.

"Being your shrink would probably turn me into one," he replied.

They sparred with brotherly banter a little while longer until Cael circled back to the show. "Not to take anything away from you, Minks, but I wish the real deal were that easy."

"Me, too. If only every case had somebody plotting for it to be solved in one night. The schemers behind our investigations would like theirs never to be cracked."

They all acknowledged her point and fell silent, each of them seeming to want some solitude. Mulling over Cael's last statement, Minka resumed her pondering about whether or not Logan's murder had any connections to Levi's pretend one. Other than his choking to death, nothing stuck out to her. She was surprised by the uncommon cause of his demise since she would've expected a more generic and typical one, like a peanut allergy. She wondered if it'd given Logan's killer an idea.

She still hadn't decided whether or not to share Logan's note with her partner, but in her clutch, it seemed to become heavier with time. Her opinion fluctuated by the moment, as she sometimes convinced herself it was necessary information and that cluing him in wouldn't be the terrible feat she initially made it out to be. Only her pride was at stake, not just because of her run-in with Shantelle but because this made them reliant on her, too. Her animosity for her had brewed for seven years, so she had a hard time suddenly considering her an ally.

Minka strived not to delve too much deeper into the past, uneager to rev up her stress again. To preoccupy her brain, she offered her tablet to them before she'd lose the connection.

Cael frowned. "I thought we agreed not to employ the Wi-Fi unless we had an emergency."

"I was afraid I was losing my child and maybe even my life. Wouldn't you deem that an emergency?"

"No, the real emergency happened after you started doing your own medical research," Wes replied.

She rolled her eyes. Before any of them asked to use it, her tablet buzzed with an email notification. "Wait! Sadie just replied to the message I sent earlier." She skimmed the words and summarized the content aloud. "An associate of hers took some of his own tests of Logan's lung tissue yesterday. She just heard back from him, and from his experience in the military, he deduced a nerve agent was at play."

"Has he narrowed it down at all?" Cael questioned.

"He can't be dogmatic without the toxicology results, but he says it resembles one of the so-called G-series nerve agents, possibly Tabun, developed by Germany in the thirties and forties."

"Nothing good emerged from Germany in the thirties and forties," Cael stated.

Wes, a biology teacher, chimed in with his chemistry knowledge. "Believe it or not, they didn't have the worst of intentions with those compounds, originally trying to make better pesticides. Once they discovered how it could affect people, though, they and other countries weaponized it. Being colorless and tasteless, it's not hard to distribute it to people."

She swallowed deeply, pondering their vulnerability to any of the crew members slipping it to them and others. She recalled Sadie's earlier findings. "It impacts the lungs, I take it?"

He nodded. "As well as the muscles. It's a pretty miserable way to die."

"How would he have contracted it?" Cael inquired.

"A number of ways," Wes said. "It's airborne, so you can get sick from being exposed to the chemical itself or even if you're around someone who's inhaled the vapors. It could be injected or put into food or water, although it loses its potency quicker if it's dissolved like that. For it to kill somebody, it must've been a high dose."

Minka scanned the message, which relayed a lot of what her husband told them. "I'm a little disturbed you're so up on your chemical warfare trivia."

They shared a chuckle before they fell silent again. Minka reeled from the knowledge she now had along with the questions that branched out from it. The similarities to the mystery experience dwindled, but both cases shared the fact of having unexpected causes of death.

After they enjoyed the moonlit setting for nearly two hours, they parted to their separate cabins and put an end to the especially long day. Entering through the door, Minka couldn't believe she was confined to the room just that morning and scared for her and Peyton's safety only twenty-four hours earlier. She savored being able to swap her gown for pajamas. Before sliding under the covers, her most aggressive of cravings, ice, hit her.

Plagued by dry mouth each time she was expecting,

she wouldn't be able to sleep without a glass of cubes on hand. With Wes taking a shower, she headed out to the ice machine in the next hallway. It wasn't her proudest of moments, passing many who were still dressed in their finest and viewing the hour to be the night's beginning while hers had clearly ended.

She rose above her humiliation and kept her sense of humor, passing by a young couple in a heated lip lock. When they glanced her way, she pointed to her bump. "Take it from me: That leads to this real quick."

Snickering over her own joke and the hesitant stares they exchanged, she filled her bucket and started back to the cabin before she recognized another well-dressed woman. To her relief, Shantelle didn't notice her as she appeared to be preoccupied with someone else—Spencer Franklin. Popping an ice cube in her mouth, Minka quietly chewed and ducked behind the corner, eavesdropping on their conversation.

"Are you sleeping any better?" Franklin inquired.

She shook her head. "I can't stop thinking about it. Everything reminds me of him, and that last time we talked, and…"

She started to sob, making her coworker embrace her. "The pain will fade, trust me."

"I don't know if I can forgive myself for the way I treated him."

"He'd want you to."

With that, Franklin planted a kiss on her cheek, and they parted ways. Observing them go, Minka could only guess if they did so as colleagues…or more.

****

Tossing and turning in the already small bed she and Wes shared, Minka's nonstop theorizing robbed them both of sufficient rest. Shantelle's conversation with Franklin replayed in her mind on a loop, beckoning for her to decode its cryptic meaning. Of all the elements that had emerged throughout the previous day, this one puzzled her the most.

Because of their history, Minka's first inclination was again to paint Shantelle to be the person at fault for her boyfriend's death. Maybe they'd fallen in love while scheming over whatever he wanted out of in the end, and she snapped when he revealed his change of heart. It wouldn't be the first time love grew cold when one party was denied what he or she wanted.

Then again, she supposed, the performer's remorse could've been due to a common lovers' spat. After all, she'd found Logan's troubling note to her before his passing, so she could've called him, understandably demanding answers. If he was as reluctant to elaborate as he seemed to be in the note, it'd be easy to imagine their discussion escalating, leading Shantelle to act in a way she'd soon regret. She no doubt hoped to repair matters the next time they spoke until she learned there wouldn't be a chance.

Minka's longtime enemy wasn't the only brow-raising piece of the equation, however; the way Franklin consoled Shantelle also struck her as suspicious. True, they'd probably worked together for a while—maybe since Shantelle was hired—and had become well-acquainted. That said, his hands-on approach wasn't any too professional or even a mere casual gesture, especially considering he was her engaged superior. In the thirteen years she'd worked with Gus Channing, they'd hugged on just a handful of occasions, and none of them were close to this level of emotion. And why would he be grieving if he hardly knew Logan, like he'd claimed to her and Cael?

There had to be a reason for it all, and in recalling the day's events, Minka stumbled on a good one. Just hours ago, she was looking for similarities between the case and the mystery act, and lying awake in bed, another possibility struck her. What if Franklin, akin to Dexter Bradley, had developed feelings for Shantelle and was driven to follow the course of the fictional psychiatrist? That way, he'd be there to comfort her during her mourning and claim his spot in her heart before anyone else could.

Her mind racing through scenarios, she'd need psychiatric help if none of them proved to be remotely true. She managed to bore herself to sleep in time but only for a couple of hours. Before six, she rose from bed to keep from robbing Wes of rest and retreated to the deck.

As the sun rose out of the sea, she contemplated the suspected method of operation employed by Logan's killer. She began to wonder if it were even plausible for a crewmate to go to such lengths. They were away from home for so many months of the year that she couldn't imagine one having the time or resources to harbor a chemical weapon aboard the ship. There were many other easier and efficient ways to off someone instantaneously. Why devise that complicated of a scheme, when the bullet they put in him later would've done the job?

They clearly wanted him to suffer. It didn't take an esteemed profiler to deduce that. It begged the question, though, of what Logan had done to merit the agonizing treatment. Even if he were a rat, that was far from the swim up the river or lead poisoning that mobsters and drug lords typically gave their betrayers. This was a specific MO, which had to be the result of a specific offense.

As she would've if she were back home, Minka revisited the notes on her tablet about the victim and tried to pinpoint anything they may have missed. While doing so, Cael appeared and sat down next to her. He yawned. "Can't you ever sleep in on vacation?"

"In case you forgot, we didn't come here for a break."

"Please, Minks, don't break my heart before eight o'clock."

His comment helped her transition well into the subject at hand. "Actually, I'm hoping to give it a jolt."

Taking the note Logan wrote to Shantelle from her tote, she gave it to her partner and allowed him to examine it. For a moment, he could only lean back in his seat and tap his fingertips on the table. Because of the crowd filtering in around them, he resorted to sign language. *This is bigger than I imagined.*

Bigger than a cruise ship? she joked.

I'm wondering. After all, somebody did follow him in hot pursuit. Even committed grand theft.

Nodding, she agreed with his speculation and added her own. *Between the note and his sudden departure, I still think he was trying to escape something that was going on here. Otherwise, why not stay aboard?*

He didn't dispute her reasoning, and they shared an unspoken resolve to unearth whatever Logan was fleeing from in the next two days. Before long, Autumn interrupted their silent strategizing, joining them at the table, soon followed by Wes. Within the hour, the ship docked at the port in Cozumel, Mexico, inciting claps and cheers from the excited passengers. As they'd worked out on Friday, Cael and Autumn would enjoy the island that morning and would relieve Minka and Wes around lunchtime. Their plan was slightly impeded, however, by the hand of Tula Hawkings.

"Aren't you coming along?" she questioned Wes once she observed the couples parting ways. "I would've figured you, of all people, would be waiting up half the night, anxious to track down your dear family."

Wes quickly—and almost too effortlessly—tapped back into his deceitful side. "I was, and that's why we're getting a later start. We're exhausted, and after Friday night, we don't want to push it with the baby. Right, honey?"

His wife enabled him with a nod, but Tula wouldn't let the issue die. "Well, is there anything we can do to help? Do you have any names? Stewy's time in the FBI gave him a knack for locating people."

"I really appreciate that, but I think it's best if we handle it. It's jarring enough to hear they have a long lost relative, without having it come from a stranger."

"Aren't you a stranger for now, at least?"

At last, he began to squirm, with his family awaiting his rebuttal with smirks. "Hopefully I'll resemble them somewhat, taking away a bit of the shock factor."

To Minka's surprise, Tula accepted the cockamamie logic, making Wes give the other three a smug grin. Cael and Autumn made their exit along with a throng of fellow tourists. The only ones to stay behind, it seemed, were those who'd partied hard the night before and were still hung over. Thus, Minka and Wes didn't have much company.

Once everyone vacated the ship, the same anxiousness she had their first day bubbled inside Minka. Yet again, she wondered if their unconventional investigative techniques would reap any success. No matter what Cael or Gus claimed about it not being a waste either way, this was her plan, and she'd be greatly disappointed and embarrassed if they didn't net any results. It was her moment to prove her instincts, and she determined to start the new day off with a lead.

Despite her nerves, she had a better grasp on the case now than she did two days ago, and she was convinced Franklin was a key to it. As always, she just needed to hunt down the evidence. Hence, her first goal of the morning was to keep track of him to the best degree that circumstances would permit. Before she could do that, though, she needed to locate him. Bound yet again by their cover of being ordinary vacationers, she couldn't ask where he was for no reason, nor could she search the entire ship for him.

After mulling the dilemma over for a moment, Minka recalled how the director was summoned the other day because of a passenger's complaint. Based on his grumbling, she gathered public relations like that was part of his job description. A devious grin crossed her lips, as she also remembered his offer to assist in keeping her comfortable. She employed her husband's cunning tactics. "Is there anything you dislike about our cabin?"

A mischievous smirk spread over his face. "That we haven't been in it with the frequency we were on our honeymoon."

She shook her head. "That won't work for the complaint desk."

"I didn't intend it for them." He winked.

"Otherwise, I did notice a little mold on the corner of the bathtub. I didn't think it was a huge deal, though."

She shared his opinion, having seen worse at hotels and even houses she'd lived in during her transitory childhood, but she had to go with it. To Wes's astonishment, she called over the first crew member she spotted and began her act.

"Excuse me, miss." She entreated a young woman who passed by them. "As you can see, I'm expecting and have to be very careful about what I take into my body. When I showered this morning, I saw a blotch of mold in our tub, and it obviously concerned me. In fact, I haven't felt well since, which is why we haven't left the ship. I'd appreciate it if someone could check on it for us. We're afraid to even go back in there."

"Of course. I'll page the custodial staff and have it cleaned right away. We could have you relocated, too, if you'd feel safer."

Unsatisfied with the simple, amiable fix, Minka upped her criticism. "I'd also like to speak with the cruise director. You can't advertise this as a family experience under these shanty conditions. My unborn child's lungs could suffer permanent damage."

"I'm sorry, ma'am. I'll get ahold of Mr. Franklin for you," she agreed but not with the same friendliness she had at first.

After she disappeared, Wes scowled at his wife. "What was that? Are your hormones really becoming this radical? Because if they are, we're going to have problems these next four months!"

"Relax. I just needed to draw Franklin here, so I can keep tabs on him through the morning."

"You're pretty sure he's involved, then?"

"I wouldn't go that far yet, but I'm less sure that he isn't involved."

Franklin must not have been far, given he was already approaching them, his expression anything but thrilled when he noticed it was Minka. Nonetheless, he put on a smile and spoke kindly to his guests. "We meet again, Mrs. …"

She used her maiden name, in case he'd remember it from their phone call. "Parker."

He feigned recognition, although he hadn't asked her name before. "Oh yes." Introducing himself to Wes and shaking his hand, he addressed them about Minka's grievance. "I understand there's a mold issue in your bathroom?"

"More like an infestation!" Minka exclaimed. She proceeded to recite the same tale she'd told his coworker. "I simply can't take chances at this stage of my pregnancy."

He assured her that he understood and made the same concessions the young woman had, agreeing to send in the janitor, and he offered them another cabin. Given that they needed to be near Cael and Autumn, she declined the latter, reasoning that if it was taken care of that morning, they'd be comfortable returning by the day's end. Franklin sighed in evident relief, and he politely excused himself, giving Minka what she wanted.

I'm going to disappear for a while, she signed to Wes.

After the last ten minutes, I'm glad.

She narrowed her eyes at him but realized how humiliated she'd be if she were in his place. Then again, she had been when facing the twisted fable he told Tula. Regardless, she followed in the director's footsteps, keeping her distance to remain inconspicuous.

Franklin proved true to his word, going to his office first to call the custodial department and tell them that another grouchy pregnant lady was whining about mold. She disliked the description, but it pleased her that she'd chosen a familiar complaint. Another matter seized her attention when she glanced up and noticed a surveillance camera, her usual ally but at that moment, an adversary. If the security desk was paying attention to it, they'd surely notice her trailing him, especially as the morning progressed.

She tried not to stare, aware it would only add to her guilt, and peered around her for some sort of reason for her to be there. The bare hallway only featured cabins, and none of them were hers. Besides that, she was around the corner from the cruise director's office, in an alcove with even more nothingness. Any semi-competent security guard should be on his way within minutes if she didn't move along or convincingly appear to be occupied.

Reaching, Minka noted the large window behind her, which, at the time, was just showing the ship docked beside them. Not caring, she went against her nature and took a selfie in front of it, cradling her belly to heighten her veneer of innocence. She snapped the shot, and stalling, she took one more before debating what to do next. All at once, her decision seemed to be made for her, at least for a second.

"Can I take it for you?" the ship's photographer offered.

"Sure," she replied, trying to conceal how flustered he'd made her.

He took her phone and waited for her to resume her

pose. "This isn't a typical setting guests choose. I don't think I've ever found anyone wanting a shot here."

"Well, I think I have one just about everywhere else. Besides, I'm getting rather warm on the deck."

He muttered an acknowledgement while taking the picture and showed it to her for her approval. "You'll have quite an album to show the kid."

Minka chuckled, agreeing with him, and thanked him for his kind assistance. He headed back toward the hallway, and he rounded the corner to enter Franklin's office. She wouldn't have thought much of it, if not for his momentary glance at her as he retreated inside. She supposed he could've been worried about her loitering in the remote area, but with her sights already set on the director, it piqued her suspicions further. She strolled that way with her eyes on her phone and closed in on the room, hoping the photographer wasn't still wary of her.

With the door three-quarters shut, she cranked up the volume on her cochlear transmitter and eavesdropped.

"This one paid off bigger than we anticipated," the photographer related. "Highest jackpot yet!"

"Desperation is a beautiful thing," Franklin replied. Minka could visualize him holding a stack of money.

"You think we ought to call it a week?"

"Absolutely not. Like I keep telling you guys, successful people don't cowardly quit just when they're peaking."

Minka willed him to continue the lesson with more details about their operation, but instead, the photographer simply gave an understanding response. She could tell the deliberation was ending and prepared to desert her spot, but she had to halt when she caught wind of Franklin's next words.

"By the way, I closed Logan's account in Nassau and cashed out his funds to divvy up. He couldn't say we didn't warn him."

Chapter Nine

Following her snooping session, Minka wasn't sure what she should—or more importantly—could do next. In a regular investigation in her jurisdiction, this was when she'd confront the persons of interest or obtain a search warrant. With no way to prevent them from running off the ship and eluding justice, she could do neither.

After meditating on what the two men had revealed, she had better insight into the players of the game, but little into the game itself. She began to theorize that their exploits might pertain to gambling, with the photographer using the terms *paid off bigger* and *jackpot*. But Franklin's reply about desperation threw her off the notion. Was he referring to his own desperation? Or someone else's?

All indications pointed to it being somebody else's, as they'd clearly profited from it. While she never liked to narrow her possibilities too prematurely, one suspicion alone occurred to Minka: extortion. Such an operation fit well in line with Franklin's comments and even reminded her of Logan's text message about them having a close call. Maybe one of their targets threatened to reverse their roles and expose their schemes.

In her contemplation, one theory led to another, like a hairline crack spider-webbing across a pane of glass. It invigorated her after days of only being more perplexed by each turn, but the seasoned detective still hit the brakes. In reality, the only crime she could accuse them of was stealing from Logan's offshore account, one few people knew existed. Drawing hasty conclusions wouldn't cut it; she needed more proof they were behind his death.

She decided to take advantage of her restored cell phone signal and call her partner while her discovery was fresh in mind. Ducking into her cabin, she recounted her past twenty minutes to Cael, who commended her for her ingenuity in the short amount of time since he and Autumn disembarked. He agreed with her deduction of their being involved in blackmail, and like her, he quickly began to dissect the assumption.

"With these high-brow passengers roaming the ship, it's not difficult to envision them jumping on that," he stated.

"Do you really think they could get acquainted with these people well enough to extort them in just a few days, though?"

"Sure. They could do research on them or simply study their habits. If a guy's onboard wearing a wedding band and has a travel companion who doesn't share his last name, it wouldn't take a genius to latch onto what's happening there."

She supposed it was true before she shifted gears to another aspect of the case. "Franklin seems to be the man in charge in this, and the photographer appears to be a minion. I want to keep a closer eye on him, but I couldn't linger around there without blowing my cover. Did you happen to notice his name?"

"Not off hand." After a pause, he shared an epiphany. *"Wait! He must be one of the superheroes.*

He's a photographer, like one of the characters listed in Logan's phone. That's probably why he used the alter ego's name, instead of using his superhero moniker."

Recalling the other contacts in the victim's phone, Minka tapped into her limited insight into comic books. "There was also a news reporter and—"

"A scientist." Cael showed off his pop culture knowledge again. *"There's an unusual duo on a cruise ship."*

Minka's mind continued to strategize who the others could be. "What about the third character, who seemed to be the leader in it all?"

"He was a millionaire who ran his family's business after his parents died."

"Why would a millionaire need to resort to an extortion scheme?"

"Even rich people can be greedy," Cael replied. *"In his case, it could have more to do with his leadership role or even how he operates in the shadows."*

"Franklin's office is in a remote corridor. Plus—" A knock on the door interrupted her.

"Maintenance," a male voice announced from the opposite side.

"I have to go," Minka said. "They're here to clean up the mold."

Cael was puzzled, having missed her impromptu performance. *"Mold?"*

She didn't have time to elaborate and answered the door. The sour-faced handyman clearly had his opinion of her before he'd even met her. She tried to dispel his view, thanking him for his service, but he didn't seem concerned with fraternizing. Taking her leave, she was still a bit lost as to how to keep the momentum going, but she soon stumbled on the answer. Posted on a bulletin board at the end of the hall was a sign, directing guests where to view the professional photos taken during their voyage.

In hopes that'd be the photographer's home base, Minka made the trek and was rewarded for her efforts, spotting him almost right away. She devised yet another scheme on the fly and tapped back into her innocent side. "While you aren't busy, could I view my family's shots?"

He pivoted toward his computer. "Absolutely."

She handed him her boarding pass card, which linked up various services they used on-board. After a series of clicks with his mouse, five shots appeared on the screen, one from their first night. The next three captured the poses before the Captain's dinner, and one showed them visiting on the deck, in which none of them had noticed the camera. The last alarmed her, revealing how many eyes could be on them at any time, but she couldn't let him sense that.

Rather, she giggled upon noticing Wes's hook in the formal ones and complimented him. "You have a real talent for capturing our personalities."

He seemed flattered. "That's always my goal."

She took a quick glance at his badge to identify his name as Nelson Riggs. "Before I order any, Mr. Riggs, is there a chance I could ask you to take some photos of my husband and me this morning, unless you're too busy? We've wanted to have some of my pregnancy, but we don't get many free moments at home."

Riggs hesitated, clearly not expecting such a request, but he didn't take long to decide. "I'd be happy to."

He wanted to finish up some edits which gave Minka time to retrieve Wes from the top deck. She gave her husband a brief summary of her plot, and he welcomed the chance to play along. His only concern, as usual, was how much it would cost.

"Will we have to pay him if you arrest him?"

Ignoring his penny-pinching, she led him back to their cabin, and once they'd ensured the maintenance man was gone, they changed into appropriate clothes. He wore a dress shirt, rolling up the long sleeves, and khakis, while she chose a floor-length sundress. For an unplanned photo shoot, it was very well handled, with Riggs taking the couple all over the ship. With so few passengers aboard, they had exclusive access to the decks, dining room, and ballroom, all making for glamorous backdrops. For a moment, Minka even forgot about the investigation and relished in the special treatment, only wishing Caela could've been involved in it, too.

She couldn't let the opportunity pass, however, so in between their final few shots, she began her inquisition, cushioning it with compliments. "You have such an astute vision for setting the scene. How did you get your start?"

"At first, it was a hobby, but once I became a photographer for my high school paper, I couldn't quit. I earned a fairly lucrative scholarship from a university that's known for its great photography program, and that led to several internships. Before I could even catch my breath from those, I found myself working for Global Expeditions."

"No way!" Wes was genuinely impressed, having used the magazine in his classes through the years, as he told Riggs. He offered a natural follow-up. "Is this a part-time gig, then?"

Tinkering with his camera lens, he didn't look up when he stated, "Nope, my days there are over. The economy didn't recover enough to spare us from lay-offs, and my lack of seniority pinned me as one of them. I applied to every other magazine I could, but nothing panned out."

Wes and Minka expressed their sympathy for his misfortune, and the subject dropped. During the conclusion of their session, Minka recapped his experience, wanting to retain every detail, and linked the similarities between him and Logan. Both were recognized for their talents early in adulthood and had promising careers, only to have them ripped away before they could enjoy it. Mulling it over, she had to wonder if the shared disappointments drove them to engage in whatever Franklin coerced them to do.

On the same line of thought, Minka also pondered if their boss, too, had been unfulfilled in his current occupation. The little he'd let on to her didn't indicate such, given he was promoted to his position, but that didn't mean it was his dream life, as Shantelle told her and Wes. After all, the muscular physique and exercise regime she'd seen glimpses of on social media could serve him well in better paying- and more desirable-professions than cruise director.

Resisting her inclination to get caught up in their backgrounds, she followed her husband back to the cabin after thanking Riggs once again with a generous tip. Before changing into her comfortable apparel, she plucked out her phone to call Gus Channing to discover that he'd already called her twice. Without listening to the voicemail he left, she pressed *send* and waited to inform him of her progress.

"Well, I've had a reasonably productive morning," she reported.

"We have, too," he related, uninterested in her news. *"We think we caught the guy who shot Logan."*

****

"What?" Cael cried when Minka divulged the latest development in Orlando over lunch on the island.

She relayed the police captain's update to the three. "I guess Emmett Bouscay remembered a distinctive scar on his abductor's arm. After some digging, Declan and Henry identified him as a rival of Logan Baris from his days as an aspiring singer. This guy accused him of plagiarizing a song he wrote, but he lost the lawsuit. That's probably why he dumped him close to the recording studio."

Cael locked his fingers and placed his hands on his head. "How did we miss that?"

"The case was listed in a stage name Logan used after his recording contract tanked," she replied. "Even so, I apologized to Gus, especially after he told me the property where Emmett was held used to belong to the jerk's family. I can't believe we didn't analyze that angle."

Cael absorbed the account for a moment and then grimaced. "Nothing beats having someone else crack your case."

Minka murmured a deflated word of agreement. After the group fell into a collective silence, Autumn addressed an intriguing issue. "What about the stolen SUV?"

"I mentioned that to Gus, too, but he didn't have an

answer yet."

"And where does the nerve agent enter the picture?" Wes inquired.

"That's another outlier. Sadie hadn't discussed that with Gus yet, so he didn't learn of it until I told him."

Cael straightened up in his seat. "Considering what you overheard Franklin saying today, I'd say this isn't over, and until it is, we have to keep an open mind."

His statement gave Minka a hint of hope, but the matter disheartened her, nonetheless. She could barely face going back to work Wednesday, now without a case because another pair of detectives solved it. In her colleagues' eyes, she had to be either foolishly hopeful or in want of a vacation but trying to make it look good.

She tried to clear her mind of her embarrassment, following Wes and Cael's advice to enjoy the rare opportunity for a break, if nothing else. While they waited to listen in on Declan and Henry's interview with the suspect, the couples explored Cozumel together, even visiting some Mayan ruins. It afforded a nice change of pace since they'd tag teamed while in Nassau and didn't even take the time to compare their separate experiences. For a trip, the excursion made for a pleasant afternoon, but for an investigation, it seemed like wasted time.

While on the bus trip from the ancient site, Minka's phone began to vibrate, and she gave Cael a sign to switch seats with Wes. She took the call from Declan, as her partner also put an ear to the phone, confusing the surrounding passengers. To their disappointment, the commotion ended up being unneeded.

"It wasn't him," Declan said without preamble.

"You're sure?" Minka demanded, unable to stand

the abruptness of the twists.

"Pretty certain. First of all, we didn't find any evidence he's been around Logan or his apartment in years. Plus, he's been in Japan for the past six months until he returned this week for visa purposes. Whether or not Emmett's real abductors knew his family owned that property, we can only guess."

"It's hard to mark that off as a coincidence," Minka replied. "Maybe they knew about Logan's beef with him and capitalized on it."

"I don't disagree," Declan said. *"Either way, you guys keep it up down there."*

She assured him that they would, wanting to tell him of her findings that morning since she hadn't bothered to relate it to Gus. Of course, she couldn't in the public setting, nor could she and Cael discuss the development. Rather, they shared an unspoken determination to get back to the ship and resume their investigation.

Minka could sense Wes's disappointment with the prospect, having only been on the island for a couple of the five hours he'd eagerly anticipated. Not wanting to rob him any further of the experience, she suggested he stay behind and continue to roam the destination. He seemed pleased with the compromise, giving her an appreciative kiss.

"Tell your birth family hello for us if you find them," Cael hollered when they parted, making his sister-in-law give a teasing punch to his ribs.

Once they were back on board *The Exquisite Marvel*, the partners agreed they needed to focus their attention on Franklin and Riggs. Now that they were together, they could each keep tabs on one, assuming they could locate them. Due to her and Wes's photo session, Minka was the natural pick to take Riggs, with Autumn joining her to maintain a casual appearance.

The ladies began their quest for the photographer at his usual post, where Minka had viewed their shots earlier. To their frustration, he wasn't there, but they did spot one of the pictures of Wes and Minka that he'd been touching up on his computer.

"If nothing else, you guys will have a beautiful album." Autumn gazed at the pose of Wes embracing her in the ballroom. "My best picture of us when I was pregnant was taken at a celebrity boxing event. I was a week from delivering and huge, and Cael's face was painted green!"

"So romantic," Minka joked.

They giggled over the memory, but still spotting no sign of Riggs, Minka's anxiety quickly returned. She realized their unexpected presence could cause alarm, especially if he caught them waiting for him while they should've enjoyed their last hours in the tropics. She debated whether to check back later until his computer dinged with a new message on a business networking site the crewmates apparently used to communicate. Minka scouted out surveillance cameras but didn't eye any, so she took the chance and lunged toward it.

"Keep a lookout," she commanded her sister-in-law.

As Autumn followed her orders, she stooped down and her adrenaline surged upon noting Franklin's name.

—*You there?*—

Unable to resist the opportunity, Minka took a seat at his desk.

—*Yeah.* —

—*I've decided on our next one: 7283. Think it'll be another big one!* —

It wasn't hard to determine that he was referring to a cabin number—hers and Wes's was 2245—and that it was clearly their latest target. She gave an affirmative response, hoping to sound convincing, and deleted the conversation from view. No longer dumbfounded on where to head, she and Autumn agreed the cabin would be on the seventh floor, one they had yet to visit. They made for the elevator.

Buzzkill greeted them the instant the doors opened and revealed that there was a reason they hadn't explored the level. Ropes crossed the entry, accompanied by an attendant, who obviously wasn't expecting any returning guests. She was immersed in her phone and iced tea when they vacated the elevator.

"Can I see your boarding passes?" she requested. Her expression was cynical, no doubt since she hadn't met them in the past three days.

"We're not staying here," Minka admitted, her mind racing, "but I was wondering who's staying in cabin 7283. We received their room service order this morning."

"Just give it back to the staff. They'll take care of it."

The fix too simple, she grasped for a way to learn the occupants' names. "I planned to, but I'd really like to send an apology note along with it. I need to know to whom to address it, please."

"We can't give out our guests' information without their consent. You can simply write your note and set it on the tray. They'll see it."

Her manner made it plain that she couldn't be persuaded otherwise, so Minka and Autumn had no other choice but to obey the order. Exasperated, Minka jabbed the button for the floor where Riggs's cubicle was located and began to text Cael. Before she finished, the elevator stopped, and Wynn McCallum joined them.

"Good seeing you again, Detective," Logan's roommate greeted her, nodding to Autumn, as well.

Minka cringed, still reluctant to clue Cael in about their run-in the day before. Autumn never learned much sign language, so Minka gestured zipping her lips and mouthed Cael's name. Her sister-in-law offered a thumbs-up, able to interrupt the message.

With that settled, Minka silently debated whether or not to enlist his help. She may have tipped him off about their motive for being there, but with their scope narrowing, it was risky to give away much more. These were his shipmates, and she didn't know him well enough to trust him not to meddle if he was friends with them. Still, with her resources limited, she couldn't ignore the opportunity that stared at her.

Just before the elevator made it to their desired floor, she triggered the emergency stop, alarming Wynn and Autumn. "Look, I need to know the guests' names in cabin 7283. I think they might be related to Logan's death."

"How? It's unlikely they were even here when he was alive. I'm afraid our rate of returning travelers is pretty low," Wynn told her.

"I can't explain. All I can tell you is this could be vital to our investigation and the safety of others."

"You said 7283, right?" He paused. "That isn't in my route, but I can try and get back to you on it."

Minka thanked him and disengaged the emergency stop, certain they were on their way to ending their trip with more than souvenirs.

****

While his family chased down leads, Wes savored his time on the beach, captivated by the waves rolling in while he ate a tamale. In his hour alone, he'd strolled through the local spots, but truth be known, this was the only one that brought him true satisfaction. The ocean had always called to him, ever since his maternal grandparents moved to Vero Beach when he was nine. He and Cael stayed with them for two weeks every summer thereafter, carving out a place in his heart.

Having forgotten to bring his swimming trunks along when he and Minka left the ship, he denied himself of his ultimate passion of surfing, but it was probably for the best. Every time Minka became pregnant, she had a heightened sense of his mortality, always making pleas for him not to do anything foolish that could render her an expectant widow. Granted, she was the one carrying the child and gunning down criminals on a regular basis, so he didn't quite follow her logic. He didn't bother questioning it anymore, however, but instead played everything safe until she gave birth…and then go out bungee-jumping to celebrate afterward!

In the meantime, Wes lounged by the water and peered at the various activities around him. A short distance down the shore, tourists were taking advantage of the outdoor massage parlor, with tables set up right by the water's edge. He snickered, reflecting on his and Minka's session yesterday, and wished they could've enjoyed the luxury here. He also noticed several of their fellow passengers traversing the beach. Griffin and Janine Garets had taken a nearby seat, having just concluded their tour of the local food eateries. A short time later, Wes nearly buried himself in the sand when

Tula and Stewart wandered in his direction, sure she'd inquire about his quest for his family. Much to his relief, they were caught up enough in the atmosphere not to notice him.

Even so, he experienced an eerie sensation of somebody watching him, a feeling he'd had twice before that day.

****

By the time cruisers began filing back on *The Exquisite Marvel*, Minka and Cael had accomplished little more with their sleuthing. As Minka discovered that morning, tracking Franklin entailed much strategy, with the director frequenting restricted areas that had more than one door. Keeping up with him was the equivalent of chasing a beaver, with one unable to determine where its dens would lead. From what they could perceive, though, Franklin spent his afternoon tending to his typical duties, not manifesting any signs of the malicious scheme underway.

On Minka's front, she didn't run across Wynn again to ask if he'd learned who was occupying the targeted cabin, but she hoped he'd hunt her down if needed. She and Autumn located Riggs back at his computer when they returned, but their discussion with him didn't go any further than her and Wes's pictures. After she ordered far more than her husband would've wished, the photographer received a phone call and gave them a dismissing nod. Thus, Minka's intent to keep her eyes on him was thwarted. When she glanced back at him typing on his keyboard, she could only hope he wouldn't realize that someone else had used it.

Wes boarded among the last of the travelers, refreshed from his solo afternoon in the sun. With everybody's return, Minka and Cael were forced back into the mold of ordinary tourists, disheartening them. The ship would be filled to capacity until they docked at Port Canaveral Tuesday morning, when they, too, would have to leave and go home. It wouldn't be easy to make the headway they needed to before then, being surrounded by hundreds of people. Even after the intriguing day, their hopes were dwindling, and the investigation started to feel like it was slowly sailing to its end.

"If we can just get enough evidence for a warrant, we can continue this back in Orlando," Cael stated while discussing their tough spot in Minka's cabin.

"Normally, Franklin's admission to emptying out the victim's bank account would be sufficient, but this ridiculous ocean has our hands tied," she said.

Wes defended the sea. "Don't take your disgust out on the ocean."

Minka apologized to her husband, then continued to think aloud, "Do you reckon I've hindered their plans for 7283 at all?"

"There's no way to guess," Cael replied.

"I wish we could get up there to warn the poor people, at least."

Wes offered a grin. "I have an idea!"

"One that won't get us court-marshaled?" his brother questioned.

He smirked. "Not if they don't have jurisdiction here."

The three passed on it, whatever it was, and they halted their plotting. To lighten the mood, Autumn chimed in and asked, "What should we do tonight?"

"I've been waiting for karaoke the whole week,"

Wes told them.

"Guess I won't need my cochlear, then," Minka joked.

Cael and Autumn agreed with the notion, and Autumn took out her activities' guide to learn the times and locations. Flipping through it, she teasingly suggested to Wes, "Or we could go to the 'Science at Sea' show. It might give you some new tricks for your classroom."

Minka snickered. "Again, sounds like I can take out my cochlear!"

The idea genuinely piqued Wes's interest, but Cael manifested even more eagerness. "Let me see that."

The others thought nothing of it, although his fascination in anything science was unusual, but he revealed his motive when he showed it to Minka. "Weren't we in the market for a scientist?"

****

Dinner dragged painfully slow that night, since the four were eager for the science show. Tula's curiosity about Wes's family was acutely grating, as she wanted every detail of his life and how he'd discovered the truth about his warped childhood. She was like a juice extractor, suctioning out even the tiniest dribble of gossip, which put his imagination to the test. For once, he sputtered, especially when she asked if he'd taken pictures of his family reunion on the island. He backed out and claimed the couple he identified proved to be the wrong people with the same name. By the end of the hour, a part of Minka actually missed Camille Paleta.

Finally, they could vacate the table and head to the program. Its first showing wouldn't start for half an hour, but the small auditorium was already open for attendees to take their seats. The host, Theo Cromwell, was on the stage, preparing his props in the mock science lab.

"Why don't you go up there and chat with him a bit?" Minka suggested to her husband.

"I don't want to bother him."

"Really?" Cael rebuked in a whisper. "For once, we're *asking* for your help with a case, and you give us a wimpy excuse like that?"

After Cael gave his brother a slight shove, Wes relented and approached the platform. All the while, Minka shuddered to imagine what he might say. She hoped he'd carry this off with the ease he did with Nelson Riggs during their photo shoot. As expected, he employed both his charm and his improvisational skills.

"Can I lend you a hand?" he offered while the man set up various implements for demonstrations. "I'm a science teacher, so I know my way around a lab."

"No, but thank you. Everything's pretty much ready for the moment," Cromwell declined. "You teach, huh? What grades?"

"High school biology," Wes replied. "The fun years."

"Oh, I'll bet. My folks both taught that age, too. They enjoyed it, but neither one shied away from retirement once the time arrived."

Wes concurred with the statement and glanced over at Minka and Cael, who signed, *More.*

"Guess you're following in their footsteps but without the adolescent drama. Not to mention the terrific locale."

"Yeah, it isn't bad. It's not exactly what I planned to be doing at thirty-eight, but at least I'm in the field."

"What are your aspirations?"

"I majored in chemistry and earned my doctorate. I landed my dream job in London before I was thirty, but I was wrongly accused of making a very costly mistake. I was fired, and because my boss—who was actually covering for a workmate of mine—carries a lot of sway in the chemist world, nobody would even accept my application after that."

Yet another tale of professional disappointment, Minka was quick to observe. Between Logan, Shantelle, Riggs, and now Cromwell, it seemed to be the cruise ship of broken dreams. It probably wasn't easy for any of them to tend to vacationers living it up all day, while they're resentful of the unforeseen twists life shaped for them. Again, she wondered if that played into their exploits and reminded herself to consult with Cael later about the possibility.

First, however, they needed proof of his involvement in this mysterious alliance, which they could only hope to expose during their final day-and-a-half at sea. They were off to a decent start, for Wes's comradery had secured him a spot as Cromwell's assistant. Others streamed in toward the start of the show, most of whom were parents who wanted their kids to have a taste of education during the summer vacation. Minka had to grin at the disgruntled munchkins' grimaces, figuring Caela, who hadn't inherited her father's scientific leanings, would share their dissatisfaction.

Cromwell even made a joke about the children's collective listlessness to kick off his discourse, but he remained enthusiastic for the rest of the presentation. With Wes's help, he illustrated several ocean facts by means of experiments. He demonstrated the differences between buoyancy in saltwater versus freshwater and modeled the effects of the ocean currents. He also included interactive segments, bringing out an array of sea creatures and plant-life for anyone to briefly examine. By the end of the production, the younger and older audience members appeared enriched and amused.

For her part, Minka didn't want to exit the room without more of an education on Cromwell's possible connection to the case. Thankfully, the scientist seemed to enjoy Wes's company and allowed them to linger while they visited. After a bit, Minka, Cael, and Autumn timidly trekked closer to the stage and joined in on the conversation. Of course, neither of the detectives cared about the science-related discussion and had their eyes searching for any and every clue that might've been visible.

With another act scheduled to begin in the next hour, their chance was dwindling away. Thus, Minka's silent hunt became rather frenzied, but she spotted nothing uncommon to the average science lab. It wasn't until Cromwell and Wes shook hands that she caught sight of exactly what topped their priority list.

In a duffle bag off to the side of the stage lay an assortment of vintage comic books.

Chapter Ten

Minka slept better than she had the night before, but she didn't awaken refreshed and at ease like most vacationers. Rather, she grappled with anxious thoughts about the new day, given how much was riding on it. They were already en route to their home state, and their return loomed. Even if they departed last among the travelers, they only had twenty-six hours to go.

She recalled Cael's comment about them only needing ample probable cause to merit further investigation, but it didn't comfort her. Right now, it seemed as though they had almost every piece of the puzzle, but they couldn't construct enough of it to decipher its design. Desperate to change that, she suggested pulling an all-nighter and monitoring the three men's whereabouts, merely to be shot down by her family for the sake of hers and the baby's health.

Still, she wondered whether or not Franklin's scheme with Riggs had transpired, despite her influence. Deep down, she realized that in a money-making venture—ethical or not—the leader would ensure it happened no matter what. Then again, the affirmative response she sent Franklin on Riggs's computer could've been sufficient, especially in the age of technology. She hoped Riggs remained in the dark and failed to play his role, thwarting whatever they plotted for the guest in cabin 7283.

She rose earlier than she had the entire week, as did Cael. They watched the sun rise together at their favorite spot on the top deck, both silent. While admiring the beauty of the dawn of their final day, she considered how their lives would change soon after the trip ended. In a few months, she'd be a working mother of two, with the many joys and challenges that such a position entailed. On the other hand, Cael and Autumn faced tests and procedures nobody wanted to undergo and potential news that could be life altering. The future held uncertainty for all of them, and the biggest help for them to get through it would be one another.

Seeming to be of a similar mindset, Cael muttered, "I hear Autumn told you about the polyps."

Minka nodded in silence, still struggling for the proper words over the worrisome circumstances. After a pause, she told him, "I'm so sorry, Cael. I appreciate you not wanting to mar my pregnancy, but I wish you'd shared it with us. We're here for you, especially in times like this."

"I know. We stayed quiet partly for your sake but for ours, too. Every time we talk about it between ourselves, the prospects become more real and scary, so broadcasting it would only make it worse. Last week, she mentioned making up a will, which I guess we should've done already, but I lost control. I cried for most of the night and could barely talk myself into going to work the next day. She's thirty-four, Minks, and Tyson's..."

He trailed off, unable to continue and not needing to. Minka could relate to the feelings all too well, both as a spouse who couldn't bear losing her mate and a mom who never wanted to abandon her young child. She could only rub his back, giving way to her own tears and despising how cruel life could be.

"I just can't be a single father. He needs his mom. She's everything to him," he said. "This must be a lot like how you felt when you imagined raising Caela without Wes."

She sighed. "Pretty much. Knowing he was out there, alive, probably made it somewhat easier. I could still have a thread of hope that, somehow, we might be reunited."

"Is that what helped you persevere?"

"To a degree, but what helped me most was you."

Appearing touched by her sentiment, he put an arm around her and gave her a squeeze. The two sat silent for a moment until he retreated back to business. "I suppose keeping our jobs wouldn't hurt matters, either. Any ideas for our game plan today?"

"We obviously need to stay apprised of Franklin's, Riggs's, and Cromwell's doings, but that isn't going to be a simple feat with the ship full of people. I'd be satisfied just to get my hands on the stolen comics."

Cael addressed their awkward standing yet again, his frustration clear. "And do what? Arrest him for theft? We're not supposed to know anything about Logan."

"It'd be a start. Maybe we could point Wynn McCallum to it, and he could confront Cromwell about it. He'd know if they should be in his possession."

He maintained his cynicism. "Involving a civilian is never wise, unless it can't be avoided. Besides, we can't risk the investigation by revealing ourselves to someone who can take advantage of it. It's bad enough having Shantelle onto us. We've miraculously avoided him up till now, and we'd be fools to seek him out on a tenuous day like this."

Minka wasn't eager to inform him that she'd already involved Logan's roommate, sensing that he wouldn't applaud her for it. Instead, she shifted the pressure back in his direction. "What do you propose we do?"

"I agree we need all the assistance we can rally, but I say we stick with those we can trust—our fellow detectives. We can tell them our suspicions, and maybe, they can dig up something on our guys that we could use here."

Minka had her doubts, given that she'd already done research of her own on Franklin, but she didn't voice her concerns. True, she may have had access to the police database, but they had resources there that weren't available five-hundred miles offshore. She and Cael agreed to split the Internet fee and composed an email to Declan and Henry, detailing their experiences with the men in question. Taking twenty minutes, they realized how much they had on each of them and yet how far they seemed to be from a solution. They read it over before they sent it off and hoped their colleagues would catch something they didn't.

Their spouses emerged from the stairway soon afterward, and the four began their day the same way they had pretty much the whole trip. Taking a while to chat, they leisurely made it over to the breakfast buffet, where many of the other guests—led by Griffin Garets—seemed determined to get the most out of their last day of inclusive meals. The kitchen staff was replenishing their rapidly depleting pans when the couples started through the line.

"Pregnant lady coming through," Griffin announced while accompanying Minka.

Embarrassed, she assured those nearby, "I'm fine

with what I have. No need to short yourselves."

"You're pregnant, too?" he quipped, patting his gut. "In all honesty, I'm just here for some juice...and everything else!"

His remark evoked a collective chuckle from the diners and staffers who overheard, his booming voice carrying across the buffet area. They'd nearly finished their breakfast when Autumn suggested they video chat with the kids since they forked over the usage charge. Embracing the distraction, Minka snagged her tablet. Once she verified that Jaclyn was logged in, she tapped the button to call her. Her mother-in-law didn't answer right away, and they were about to disconnect by the time she finally did.

When she switched on the camera and unmuted her microphone, applesauce covered her face, while Tyson wailed in the background and Caela was snapping a list of complaints. "Please, tell me the ship's docked a day early."

"Nah, Mom, we were stranded and have to wait on the Coast Guard to rescue us," Wes told her.

"Maybe some pirates will find you again, dear," Jaclyn replied.

"Wait," Minka interrupted. "How did you know his ludicrous cover story?"

"He told that tale to his second-grade class," Jaclyn stated. "The craziest part is his teacher bought it! She even asked me to present her with his birth certificate."

Minka elbowed her husband. "You need to get some new material."

He beamed. "Why? It always works."

In an effort to help her endure one more day with the children, each set of parents talked with their youngster one-on-one. Cael and Autumn had the hardest time calming Tyson, who couldn't grasp the concept of being unable to touch them. Caela related several of her grumbles, mainly over her nana's menus, but she settled down after a while, especially after Minka held the tablet to her tummy. The big sister told Peyton to keep popping. Once the call ended, they sighed in relief over the little ones' better attitudes but speculated about what the day at home would bring.

Minka could only hope disrupting the families' routines would pay off, but her optimism for the investigation continued to fade. Cael's plan didn't include any solid course of action for them, apart from contacting Declan and Henry. Once they sent the email, they couldn't do anything but wait for a response, if one came at all. They didn't have a clue of what was transpiring in Orlando at the moment, so the detectives could be preoccupied with a more pressing case of their own.

Not helping matters, Wes and Autumn seemed equally weary of the sleuth work, although it was the reason they took the trip. Minka couldn't help being perturbed by their apathy but then recalled her feelings earlier that morning about their changing lives. This was the final day they had just to be couples, not parents, employees, or, in Autumn's case, a patient. Once again, history repeated itself, as Minka recollected one memory from her honeymoon that time had nearly erased...

After only twenty-four hours of knowing they had a baby on the way, Minka already had her stroller, crib, and car seat selected from a magazine in the gift shop. Her anxieties from the afternoon before passed, mostly because of her husband's reassurances that they'd make the needed adjustments for their growing family. Hence, she dove right into maternity, buying every magazine with a child on it and began planning.

"Do you like Skyler or Calvin for a boy?" she questioned Wes in the pool.

"I'm partial to Hercules."

She shook her head, rebuking herself for expecting a serious response after his pick for a daughter's name was Zelda. Floating for a moment, she opted to close the subject, soon noticing a slight rise in her middle. "Wes, I think I'm showing! Look!"

She framed her abdomen for him, which he scrutinized with doubtful eyes, and he gave a perfunctory reply, "Maybe so."

Detecting his lack of enthusiasm, she tried to keep her cool, but her worry quickly overtook her. "Don't you want this baby?"

"Of course, I do, honey." He waded over and took hold of her. "I'm thrilled about it, but we have seven months to decide on names and furniture and to watch both of you develop. This is our last day of our honeymoon, a week we'll never get back. We'll be back home tomorrow, grocery shopping, paying bills, and unpacking more of your endless shoe closet, which you need to start condensing for the baby's clothes."

"How dare you," she teased.

"Let's just be beautiful bride and insanely happy groom for today, and tomorrow we can begin our road to parenthood."

Much like she did then, Minka endeavored to please Wes and give him the break he needed from reality. Ironically, they ended up in the pool, along with seemingly half of the other cruisers. It was too crowded for her tastes, given she was the most pregnant woman there, but she maintained good spirits for her family's sake. Even so, she climbed out before the rest of them and headed back to the cabin.

While she changed clothes, her gaze lingered on the clock, and each time she glanced, she became more apprehensive. Eleven o'clock approached, and they hadn't tried to catch a glimpse of one of their suspects. Once dressed and finished with her makeup, she checked her email, only to discover nothing but spam. In that moment, she concluded no one else was concerned about getting justice for Logan, and it rested on her shoulders to act in his—and quite possibly others'—interests.

To her advantage, she still had an in with Nelson Riggs since he'd promised to have her and Wes's photos printed by mid-day. She reckoned it may have been a little early, but being on her own, she embraced the convenience of not having to clear it with anybody. Thus, she took the elevator down a level and trudged through the crowd to his office. He wasn't there, but that didn't mean his office was empty.

"Oh, hi, Mrs. ..." Franklin greeted her, clumsily scooting away from Riggs's computer.

"Parker," she reminded him again. "I was looking for Mr. Riggs. He took some pictures of my husband and me, so I came to pick them up."

"Sure. Well, he's out snapping some shots right now, but you could probably catch him in about an hour. He'll be back for lunch," the director explained before he appeared to feel the need to justify his own presence. Becoming rather fidgety, he added, "I needed to find a file that couldn't wait."

Minka gave a polite nod, enjoying the sight of him

rattled.

He stood from the office chair and wobbled toward her. "Are you satisfied with your cabin now? Is the mold gone?"

"Yes, your custodian did a superb job. My little one and I extend our deepest gratitude."

He failed to conceal how relieved he was to end the awkward exchange. "Happy to help."

She evaluated his body language as he trotted away and debated between following him or trying to sort out what his business was on Riggs's computer. She didn't hesitate for long, but by the time she pivoted to see which direction he headed, he'd vanished from view amongst the thick, oblivious throng of passengers. Meanwhile, nobody milled around the vacant office, lending an opening she couldn't refuse.

When she bent down to the screen, it showed the same business networking page it'd featured the day before. There were new posts, however, swapped between the two.

Franklin initiated the conversation the night before.
—*Did it go well?*—
Riggs responded three minutes later.
—*What?*—
—*Phase one. I gave you our mark.*—
— *No, you didn't.*—
—*I did, and you said you'd handle it.*—

The discussion ended there, but Minka deduced they hadn't settled the confrontation. At best, Franklin was snooping around his ally's computer to figure out if and why he was unaware of his orders. At worst, he'd realize that it was because of Minka.

****

Headed to lunch with her family, Minka didn't have much of an appetite, as she continued to contemplate Franklin's messages to Riggs. Now certain that she had indeed put a snag in their scheme, it didn't give her the gratification she would've anticipated. Instead, it left her worried for both the investigation and her safety. She wasn't sure if there was a way they'd determine her involvement, but finding Franklin actively pursuing it revealed his fortitude.

After an hour of internal deliberation, a couple of stabs fired up around her middle again, tamer than the ones she'd experienced Friday but definitely there. Reminded that more was on the line than the case, she released a few deep exhales and sought to quell her unsettling thoughts.

Once they'd filled their plates at the lunch buffet, the Averys threaded their way through the hungry crowd, spotting Stewart Hawkings in it. With enough distance between them to pass him by without appearing rude, Minka intended to do exactly that until her cunning husband had to call him over.

"How do you do, Stew?" he greeted him with the corny expression he'd adopted on their second night. Regardless of how many times he said it, Minka still closed her eyes and blushed.

Stewart never seemed too entertained by it, either, and this afternoon was no exception. "All right, I suppose."

Since he didn't have a great sense of humor, his dreariness didn't strike anyone as unusual, so Wes kept his tone upbeat. "Where is the missus?"

"Sick in bed. We think she caught a bug on the island. Histoplasmosis is rampant in southern Mexico."

With his arrogance on full display, Minka couldn't feel too sorry for him or his flamboyant wife, but Wes conveyed his concern. On the contrary, Minka rejoiced inside at the prospect of not having to deal with Tula for the day. If she was fortunate, she may not even run into her before they all exited the ship.

While they munched on their meals, Minka's focus continued to waver back to Franklin's ire. She did her best to conceal her angst, but she must've failed, as Cael called her out about it.

"What happened after you left the pool?" he questioned her when Wes and Autumn roamed off to refill their drinks.

She stuck with the obvious. "I changed clothes."

"Yeah, and personalities. For starters, you haven't eaten this little since you were battling morning sickness, and secondly, you've never been this quiet. Drop the act, Minks."

Called out, she relented. "I went to retrieve our photos from Riggs and instead found Franklin in his office. He was acting strangely, snooping around on the computer, so I did some of my own after he walked away. Turns out, he's on to the fact that Riggs wasn't the one who replied to his command yesterday, and I think he's set on figuring out who was."

"And this surprises you?"

She had similar thoughts, but his tone and cocked eyebrow didn't make it easy to swallow. Nonetheless, she admitted, "This isn't going to make my highlight reel of professional achievements, okay?"

Cael had to chuckle over her blunt self-awareness, but he didn't wallop her with more blame. "You said there wasn't any surveillance around, right? How else are they going to realize it? They aren't about to dust the keys for fingerprints. It's a second-rate cruise ship."

"Where a member of its crew ended up murdered because of the goings-on, at least according to us."

He acknowledged that her point was valid but still discouraged her from letting her mind race uncontrollably. "Just don't get ahead of yourself. We have one day left, so I doubt that's enough time for them to catch on to us."

"We've figured out a lot about them in the past twenty-four hours, and I hope to uncover even more in the next."

He shrugged. "We're trained investigators, and they're not. Have you heard from Declan and Henry?"

She drew out her tablet from her tote bag. Just as she tapped on her email app, a video call popped onto the screen from Declan. Eager to learn the reason behind it, Minka sprung up and sat down beside her partner as she answered it.

With barely any preamble, the detective reported, "Well, you guys were right to have your suspicions, primarily about Cromwell. He made quite the stir over in the UK when the lab he worked for accused him of using Tabun, a toxic nerve agent, instead of Gallium in a research study on cures for malaria. He blamed it on the fact that both chemicals are commonly labeled 'Ga', but his employers didn't buy it."

"He claims he was set up," Minka stated.

"So we read." Henry appeared in the corner of the screen. "It wasn't a very convincing tale since the lab doesn't keep a supply of Tabun on hand. Apparently, it's pretty rare."

Wes, who'd just taken his seat, nodded in agreement

to the fact.

Before either of them could ask the obvious, Declan continued, "The local police recovered an invoice for it in his house and confirmed that it was paid for with his credit card."

"Why would he do this?" Cael wondered aloud.

"At the time, they were competing with another lab for a contract with a drug company. Rumor had it their competitor paid Cromwell off to derail them, and it worked. They were sued by test subjects who suffered seizures and various reactions because of the mix-up, and the other lab landed the deal. There was never proof of the two working together, but his company fired him due to all it'd cost them," Declan informed them.

"And now, it's the suspected cause of death in his coworker's murder," Minka declared.

****

Following their video chat with Declan and Henry, the matter spun through Minka's head like a scratched record. The chances of a rare chemical, with which Cromwell had infamous history, coincidentally killing his coworker, were beyond astronomical. Plus, if his former lab's account were true, it revealed that the chemist was willing to harm others for his financial gain. Combining his knowledge, callousness, and greed, he had what it took to be a successful blackmailer.

Recounting her earlier thoughts about their possible extortion scheme, Minka began to further theorize about their individual roles. Riggs, she realized, was a prime candidate for such an operation, for his position would be ideal for capturing guests' dirty little secrets and proceeding as expected. Logan could get acquainted with them through his serving duties and even through his performing; she'd observed several of the entertainers engaging with audience members after the show Thursday night. With Franklin the apparent leader, where did that leave Cromwell?

He carried no camera, nor did he appear to be the chummy type, but she had to guess he was employed for his brain. But why? He was a scientist, not a psychologist, who could've determined what they could use or how they could coerce people into giving them what they wanted.

Or could he?

"What if he's the weapon?" Minka told Cael while the four traversed the on-board mini-golf course.

Her suggestion caught him off guard. "What?"

"Cromwell—what if his part in this was to develop their means of enforcement? Blackmailers need a threat of some kind. Otherwise, there's no reason to pay them off. With these guys pretty much confined to the ship, there's little power they have over their marks once they leave. It'd only make sense they did something here to make them cooperate. What if it's endangering their health?"

"What are you saying?" he questioned.

"Could they be using Tabun or some other chemical on their targets? Or at least threaten them with it?"

Cael paused, mulling over the possibility. "Logan died from it. Do you really think they could get away with carting dead passengers off the ship?"

"They could administer a smaller dose," she replied. "They wouldn't want them dead and unable to meet their demands."

He deferred to his brother. "Does that seem like a plausible scenario?"

Wes frowned. "Dealing with chemical weapons is risky, not to mention intricate. You have to take so many precautions not to get poisoned by it as the one who administers it. I'm not sure you could run such an operation on a floating petri dish without being exposed right away."

"But Logan had to contract it from somewhere," Minka said. "How long before he died would he have ingested it?"

"I can't say," Wes admitted. "Again, it depends on what method his killer used to transmit it to him."

The conversation ended there, with Cael's turn to putt rotating back around and Minka's following. Her overwhelmed mind affected her stroke, resulting in the worst hole of her game. That frustration evaporated the instant she straightened up and caught sight of Wynn in the distance.

Desperate to get over to him, she once again used her pregnancy to maneuver matters, extending her belly to appear needier. "My bladder must be this child's teddy bear because he or she keeps squeezing it. I'll meet you guys at the next hole."

Back to battling the thick crowd, Minka cut through numerous groups and couples en route to Wynn, joking to herself that she'd truly have to pee by the time she made it. With his back to her once she closed in on him, she waited to approach him until he finished speaking with another passenger. Spinning around, he spotted her immediately and wandered in her direction, but he didn't appear to be bursting with news for her.

"I was hoping to run across you," he related, giving her hope. "I wish I had a better update, though. The guests in the cabin you inquired about have their names sealed."

"You can do that?"

"If you're really important or well-known, you can. It could be a celebrity, politician, or nowadays, a reality show star, who doesn't want to risk fans—or haters—finding out they're aboard. Their identities are on a need-to-know basis. I'm quite surprised by it, to tell you the truth. I've never been aware of it happening here."

The information helped her more than he realized, for it fit perfectly with her speculations. Such an elite traveler would be a sure candidate for blackmailing, and she suspected Franklin would be privy to the information. If the extortion did involve infecting the mark with a chemical weapon, it'd make sense that he'd wait until the latter part of the trip to strike. The person would be more frantic to exit the ship alive. Plus, he or she would have more clout and perhaps more gumption to expose their schemes. The quicker they could nab their money and get the target off the ship, the safer their operation remained.

Sorting through her hypotheses, Minka didn't want to squander her opportunity with Wynn and remembered to question him, "Did you ever locate Logan's comic collection?"

He shook his head. "I'm sorry to say I haven't."

She debated how much to disclose before she gave him a vague follow-up. "Was he close enough to anybody here to give it as a gift to them perhaps?"

"Absolutely not. Even his girlfriend, whom he was about to ask to marry him, was barred from touching most of his books."

His mention of Shantelle intrigued her, and she feigned ignorance to sniff out his opinion of the relationship. "Does she work here, too?"

"Sure enough. They performed together, and Logan was crazy about her from their first rehearsal. He finally mustered the nerve to ask her out over the winter, and they were inseparable from that day forward. Her name's Shantelle, and I can arrange for her to meet with you, if you'd like. I can guarantee she'd be more than eager to help you."

Minka thanked him but reminded him of their need for anonymity. Recalling the dancer's interaction with Franklin, she asked another carefully worded query, "Did anyone else have eyes for her...or even him? Could someone have been jealous of what they had?"

"It didn't appear so to me, anyhow. Shantelle has dated a couple of guys during her time here, but I don't think her other relationships grew too serious. Fraternizing on the job isn't unheard of in this business."

She wasn't surprised, given that the majority of the staff was under thirty-five and the ship was their main means of social interaction. Taking her leave, she pondered the mingling amongst the coworkers and reflected on the possibility of jealousy being behind Logan's murder. She still deemed it plausible, but what she'd witnessed between Franklin and Riggs convinced her that more lay behind this than a jilted lover. On the contrary, she had to assume a dangerous plot was taking place around the vessel, and the sight of Franklin staring stoically at her reinforced her conviction.

Chapter Eleven

Upon returning to the mini-golf course, Minka endeavored to remain as normal as possible, aware Cael would notice a change in her demeanor. She didn't plan to reveal her run-in with Wynn since he didn't approve of her consulting with him. They didn't need to be arguing over their conflicting methods on such a crucial day. After all, Wynn hadn't shared much game-changing intel. While it impressed her to learn the cabin Franklin targeted contained a VIP guest, the only part that mattered was trying to save him or her.

She may have already done so, but she feared it wouldn't last. The tone of Franklin's instant message, as well as the steely expression he leveled her way, didn't indicate that he was shrugging off his thwarted agenda. Minka just wished she knew if he'd become aware of her part in obstructing his designs and if she should spend the rest of the day in her room. Being the detective she was, however, she couldn't cowardly forfeit these final hours of investigating even then.

Continuing to follow her family's lead, Minka finished her game of putt-putt in third place, happily beating out her husband. After that, they explored the areas of the ship they hadn't yet toured. The crowd was dense everywhere, making her wonder how there were enough cabins to fit that many bodies. To their amusement, the least packed floor was the casino, which apparently filled up later than three in the afternoon. None of them were the gambling type, but the glitzy room called out to them.

For her part, Minka wasn't too impressed. "Drunks smoking cigarettes and yelling out profanities because they lost a year's salary—no, thank you."

"You stereotype everything!" Wes accused his wife.

"I've seen everything. Cael and I have been in numerous casinos in our career, and they're all the same."

"Sounds pretty stereotypical, if you ask me," Wes teased.

While considering where to go with their repartee, her eyes caught a glimpse of a familiar figure. She did a double-take, which confirmed that it was Stewart Hawkings. Standing at the ATM, he appeared to be withdrawing some fun money. Though it was a common sight, something about it didn't sit right with Minka.

She pointed him out to the others. "I wouldn't take him to be a high roller."

"Who knows how many personalities the dude has," Cael joked.

Keeping him in her sights, she couldn't dismiss it that easily. "He was so brokenhearted earlier about Tula. I can't believe he'd be in the mood for blackjack."

"He hits me as a craps guy," Wes said. "He probably has tension to relieve, with a sick wife and all, and there's no better way to do it than rolling dice."

She raised her brow, suspecting he'd done more than lounge by the pool the morning she was bedridden. "You sound like you have experience with it."

"How do you think I paid for our massage?" he confessed with a grin.

She gave him an eye roll before Cael made an observation. "Looks like you were right, Minks. He's not hitting the tables."

Stewart passed the casino entrance and headed for the elevator. The guys and Autumn resumed their pace, acting as though it was a moot issue, until they glanced back and realized Minka hadn't moved.

"Can't we just look around for a few minutes?" Wes begged her. "I sort of had tunnel vision the other day."

Ironically, that's how she felt at the moment. "I'll be right behind you. I want to check on something."

Inciting confused expressions from the three, she trailed off in the opposite direction and stayed focused on Stewart. Requesting cash may not have been unusual, but it seemed strange to trek down to this level just to do that, considering there was an ATM on every floor. Plus, he appeared tense and quite stilted…even for him. Whether she was making too much of it or not, the scene riveted her, and she at least wanted to scope out his next move.

Thankfully, nobody else awaited the elevator, and as he stepped on, she concentrated on what the screen above the doors revealed his destination to be. Despite the fact that a part of her was expecting it, she still caught her breath when the number seven flashed across.

Could he and Tula be the guests in 7283?

****

Weeding her way through the gamblers, Minka was hardly looking for her family, lost in contemplation over her newfound theory. On one hand, she considered it a longshot and figured Cael would deem it such, too. At the same time, she couldn't believe they didn't make the connections earlier. Tula ended up sick right when they were suspecting that Franklin's team was poisoning passengers, and with her showy style and nature, she was the ideal mark. No wonder Franklin expected it to be *another big one.*

As her confidence in her theory mounted, her internal checks and balances system weighed out all the variables. Top on her list of doubts was that the couple's names would be sealed since they didn't seem to fit the criteria Wynn had relayed to her. True, they clearly had money. That said, whatever Stewart really did for employment—besides working with the FBI and inventing the Internet—didn't put them at risk for fanfare disrupting their time. With both of them delusionary egotists, however, she reckoned that they could profess a bigwig status and pay to get it.

Regardless, Minka decided she should at least inform Cael that the couple resided on the same floor as Franklin's target since there was a definite link. Once she spotted her partner over the roulette wheel, she reckoned he wouldn't be in the mood to strategize. The noisy environment didn't create for it, either. After scanning the area, she realized it pretty much met the expectations she expressed earlier. The permeating smell of cigarette smoke snapped her into protector mode, and her hand fell to her middle, as if it would shield her little one from the toxins. By the time she tracked down Wes, she was ready to retrace her steps to the exit.

"Seen enough?" she hollered, trying to overpower the sound of his slot machine.

She didn't succeed. "What?"

She took the visual approach and signed, *You ready to go?*

No way! Look at my winnings!

She shifted her eyes to the tray at his knees and guessed his grand total to be under five dollars. *I'm leaving.*

Why?

The baby, she reminded him, motioning to the surrounding smokers.

He conceded, tenderly touching her belly, but he begged, *Ten minutes?*

She agreed to meet him out front, certain that he would linger much longer. Her husband may not have been a regular gambler, but he did have a weakness for taking risks. She could only hope he'd be able to suppress that while they still had money in the bank.

With her mind focused on business, she wanted to retrieve her tablet from their room to check for any updates from Declan and Henry. Figuring she'd have time before Wes tore himself away from the slot machine, she retreated to the elevator. During her wait, the Garrets joined her.

Minka engaged them in conversation. "You two hit it big?"

"Nah, the only food in there are the cherries on the machines," Griffin drolly replied. "Every time I tried to take a bite, they spun away."

She and Janine shared a giggle before the elevator's doors opened. Four others stepped in with them, and being in the back, Minka and the Garrets had to announce their desired floor to those ahead of them. Minka's anxiety began to ease, especially in the presence of such a character like Griffin, but for once, he reawakened her restlessness.

"Seven, please," he declared, clueless of what the statement would mean to the detective.

With perked ears, she devised a way to make use of her newfound assets, casually addressing them, "Up with the high-class, huh? Nice! My sister-in-law and I wanted to explore up there, but we were clearly unwelcome. From what we could see, though, it was pretty swanky."

"It sure is," Griffin replied with satisfaction. "We normally wouldn't splurge like this, but I decided we both deserved a week of luxury after three decades of public service."

Minka expressed her wholehearted agreement, after which Janine seemed to read her mind. "Would you like to accompany us and take a peek around as our guest?"

"I don't want to interrupt your afternoon…"

"We were just going to rest up for dinner." Janine shrugged. "Griffin suffers from chronic food coma."

"And they can't figure out the cause!" he added.

Another murmur of chuckles filled the air before the doors opened to the prestigious deck. Minka didn't take any steps forward until Janine entreated her to join them, evoking a smile to her lips as she sauntered past the security guard who'd denied her and Autumn entry. Following the couple, she noted that they were going in the direction of cabin 7283, but they stopped short of it, at 7271. She figured they were only six doors away, with two on each side, but the suites were spaced far enough apart that it was at the opposite end of the hall.

While she schemed how to get close, she tried to be a gracious visitor, praising the resplendent room. More than double the size of her and Wes's cabin, it was divided into a bedroom and living area, which even had an adjoining breakfast nook accompanied by a small kitchen. The touch that stood out most of all, of course, was the attached balcony over the water.

After taking a moment to admire the view, Minka decided it was time to excuse herself, despite not attaining what she'd been seeking. Another fortunate happenstance delayed her when Janine mentioned needing to retrieve their laundry.

"Laundry service had to be the one thing my dear husband refused to pay for this week." She sighed, shaking her head when Minka was making her way out. "It's also the only thing in which he doesn't have a part. Coincidence?"

"It has to be," Minka teased.

"I handed you the bag," Griffin said.

Catching sight of the directory sign, Minka realized the laundry room was near cabin 7283, and she attempted to tag along. "I'd love to help you."

"Oh, I'm fine, but I appreciate the offer. You should enjoy your last day without housework. I'm sure you'll be doing plenty once that baby's here."

"Exactly, and I need to condition myself. After five chore-free days, I'm scared of becoming too spoiled."

To her delight, Janine accepted her reasoning and proceeded to lead her along. Still endeavoring to keep a casual front, she made small talk during their stroll, but her eyes absorbed everything around the suspicious area. When they passed 7283, the door was, not surprisingly, closed and blended in with all of the others. Had she been alone, she may well have stopped in front of it to discern if she could hear or sense anything, but she had to keep her cover for now.

Despite its elegant surroundings, the laundromat was fairly common, with the exception of the large-screen television hanging on the wall. Once she started helping her new friend unload the dryer and fold the clean clothes, Minka discovered that there was more truth in her joke about becoming spoiled than she wanted to admit. She'd packed her and Wes enough outfits to last the entire voyage, so she hadn't done the all-too-familiar task since the day before they departed. Such a short absence wouldn't have affected her under ordinary conditions, but her ever-changing body reminded her of its decreasing agility. She laughingly needed to ask for Janine's assistance in rising from her crouched position.

"I think Wes will be chipping in a bit more than normal these next few months," she joked in an effort to conceal her embarrassment.

"So, a baby is what it takes, then? Wish somebody had clued me in on that twenty-five years ago!"

"Believe me, one trimester and maybe a week after birth is the most you'll get," Minka told her. She didn't want to overstep her bounds as a relative stranger to Janine, but her prior statement prompted her to timidly ask, "You and Griffin decided not to have children?"

"My health made the choice for us," she replied in a somber tone. "I needed a hysterectomy in my early thirties. It was incredibly difficult to accept, but he and I have enough love for each other that we're content in our small family. Besides, Griffin's the equivalent of two kids!"

Minka expressed her sympathy for the sad turn of events and couldn't help but think again of Autumn and Cael's situation. She wished they could hear Janine's positive outlook, but she appreciated it'd be wrong to share their private matter. Instead, she strived to store away the sentiments for the appropriate time, which she hoped never arose.

Moseying back out into the hallway, Minka brushed

aside her personal concerns and again paid close attention to the targeted cabin. She caught her breath when she spotted a housekeeper at the door, holding the gown Tula had worn on Captain's Night, to return it from the dry cleaners. The woman made repeated knocks, but with them going unanswered, she eventually gave up and hung the dress back on the caddy. Minka and Janine, who was oblivious to the scene, passed her and the cart. Now sure it was the Hawkings's room, the detective continued to glance back to ascertain if anyone ever emerged. Once they returned to Janine and Griffin's suite, she thanked them for their kind invitation and took her leave.

Even so, she had a hard time not taking another gander down the hall since she had no hopes of making it back to the secure floor. Giving in to her urge, she took a few steps in that direction, but upon spotting Riggs round a nearby corner, she retreated to a cubby where a vending machine—and ironically, an ATM—stood. Peeking out the doorway, she observed him at the Hawkings's door, an envelope in hand, and doubted he was there to deliver pictures…or at least not the type they would've ordered.

Unlike when the housekeeper arrived, the guests granted Riggs immediate entry, and the door quickly shut behind him. Minka made sure nobody lurked around before continuing toward the room and momentarily stopped beside it, hoping to hear something. Regardless of how high she increased the volume on her transmitter, silence resounded on the other side of the wall. Still, she couldn't flee the corridor with the seemingly crucial event unfolding, so she scurried back to the laundry room, a better vantage point.

Not long afterward, the photographer exited the

cabin holding the same envelope, which was thicker than before. Considering their earlier discoveries, it took Minka no time to figure out that it contained cash. Judging by the thickness of it, she deduced the large sum was too much to withdraw from one machine. Franklin called it right when he predicted it to be a *big one*.

****

Wes consulted his watch and concluded he'd surely exceeded the ten minutes he requested of Minka and figured he'd better not push it any farther. On instinct, he checked his phone for messages from her before he recalled the lack of cell service. He pictured his pregnant wife waiting outside a casino she hadn't wanted to visit in the first place and didn't look forward to confronting the consequences. Just the same, he realized they'd only worsen the longer he delayed.

Thus, he joined the line to cash out his winnings, even if they were under fifty dollars. The wait was fairly long, with everyone wanting to claim theirs before the cruise's end, and Wes nearly gave up on it several times due to his small prize. In the end, however, he reasoned that it would incense Minka even more to have waited for him to emerge with empty hands. As it was, he'd lost almost four times what he won.

He met up with Cael and Autumn along his trek out and told them he'd be with Minka. When he made it outside the entrance where he suspected she'd be, he perused the lobby for her but didn't spot her anywhere. He questioned a few in the area, in hopes her pregnancy would draw somebody's notice, but he only received confused expressions. He'd just started up the stairs to check their room when a crew member approached and stopped him.

"Mr. Avery?"

"Yes," Wes affirmed, a knot forming in his stomach.

"You need to come with me. Your wife's in labor, and it's real this time!"

****

Minka rode the escalator back to the lobby in front of the casino, which appeared just as it had before her adventure upstairs except for different occupants—none of whom was Wes. Not surprised, she took a seat on one of the benches, somewhat relieved to get off of her feet and digest what she'd witnessed upstairs. She resented not being able to storm into Stewart and Tula's room to demand answers and to uncover what kind of condition they were in when Riggs exited. For once, Minka eagerly anticipated their dinner with the two.

She continued to wait with patience for her husband, albeit a bit annoyed, but after half an hour had passed, she rose to go and hunt for him. Thankfully, Cael and Autumn emerged before she entered, and she grasped her partner's elbow to seize his attention.

"Is Wes still in there?"

He gave her a puzzled frown. "No, he left about forty-five minutes ago. He told us he'd be with you."

"He must've come out right before I arrived. He's probably back in the cabin." She made the hasty assumption, more interested in reporting her findings to Cael. "You'll never guess where I've been."

While they moseyed toward their rooms, she recounted the hour's events, ignoring his shaking head over her antics. Aside from his misgivings about her methods, he agreed with her theory that Riggs was there to collect money he and his comrades had extorted from the couple. He shared her quandary of what could be done about it.

Remaining in synch with her, he suggested what she'd already wondered. "Maybe it's over. They clearly received their wage."

"It may be over for Tula and Stewart, but it probably isn't for future travelers. When we leave tomorrow, another crop of vacationers will be boarding this ship and may end up being new targets. We have to find something solid to get these money-hungry yahoos behind bars."

A verbal concurrence wasn't necessary from Cael, as she could tell his head was spinning at the same pace as hers. No one could be trusted, lending them no opportunity to enlist the help they truly needed. Minka had already gone rogue and implored Wynn for assistance, and thus far, it'd yielded few results.

Just when confusion and exasperation consumed her, they became further confounded by Wes's absence from the bedroom. After checking the shower, Minka concluded they'd have to either wait longer or have him paged over the intercom. Because they hated to draw unnecessary attention to themselves, they opted to give him a bit more time. With each minute that passed, their anxiety level rose higher and higher.

After half an hour, they ventured out of the room, checking Cael and Autumn's cabin for good measure. When they didn't locate him there, they started toward the main concierge desk to request the dreaded summons. Along the way, they encountered Shantelle. Minka never would've beseeched her help, but to her surprise, Shantelle offered it in an unexpected form.

Her gaze landed on Minka, but on this occasion, they shone with concern. Her fingers even brushed

Minka's wrist. "Was it another false alarm?"

Everything about this baffled her. "What are you talking about?"

"I ran into Wes downstairs, and he was rushing to the first-aid room because you were in labor."

"That's news to me," Minka said.

"Where would he get that idea?" Cael asked Shantelle.

Shantelle gestured to Minka. "I assumed straight from the source, but I see that's not the case. The cruise director, Spencer Franklin, was accompanying him."

Minka and Cael glared at each other, but neither let on their suspicions to Shantelle. Stunned by the development, Minka couldn't cook up an excuse, but thankfully, her partner managed to. "Maybe someone confused Minka with another babymooner. We'll head there now, but you can tell him Minka's fine and will be waiting in their cabin if you spot him again."

She assured them that she would. After she ventured out of earshot, Minka muttered to Cael, "Franklin must've figured out I was the one who was on Riggs's computer. I caught him glaring at me earlier."

"Wes has known your suspicion of him, though," Autumn spoke up. "Wouldn't he realize it could be a trap?"

Cael showed off his sarcastic side. "This is my brother, babe. You've met him, right?"

"Plus, my close call Friday night probably impaired his reasoning ability," Minka defended her husband, figuring Franklin learned of it and exploited it. Her wrath getting the better of her, she was reminded of the alarming instance by a sharp pain striking her, compelling her to sit down on a nearby bench.

"Easy now," her brother-in-law cautioned. "We don't want Franklin's tale to come true."

The three fell silent, allowing her to take a few cleansing breaths before another disturbing possibility occurred to her. "Who says we can trust her, anyhow? Cael, you tipped her off about my scare, so she could've staged this. Or maybe she's fabricating this altogether, and she and Franklin's squad just snagged my husband with whatever mechanisms they have at their disposal."

Cael crouched down and paused for a beat. "Her concern seemed genuine. Plus, I can't picture her colluding with them if she really loved Logan as she claimed."

"But I saw her hugging Franklin, and—" Another spasm jabbed her, which she tried to conceal with a yawn.

Her act didn't deceive Cael. "For your sake and Peyton's, you need to calm down. You and Autumn should head back to the room, and I'll start searching for Wes at the first-aid room."

"No, I'm coming, too," Minka protested and stood, but she automatically grabbed her back when a couple more spasms jarred her.

"Sure, you can. Who needs that insignificant third trimester, anyhow?" He ignored her scowl. "The three of us scouring the ship for him would draw attention. If I'm by myself, I can simply act like I'm concerned if you had an episode. People will accept that easier."

She conceded to his logic, for the sake of both the investigation and her welfare. As they made their way to the cabin, Minka grappled with conflicting emotions, although she let none of them on to Autumn. While they idly discussed nursery ideas and pediatricians, she stewed over the developments she'd withheld from Cael and how they may have factored into their present situation. Her main worries revolved around Wynn and if he—even accidentally—exposed them to his crewmates. Or, she wondered, did her other antics reveal too much? Had Franklin been aware of her tailing him the previous day?

Regardless, she found it safe to assume one or more of her acts of desperation had led to her husband's capture, and she could barely cope with the notion. For years, she'd held it against him for the risks he'd taken that led to his fleeing for his life before she had Caela, but now, she put him in danger of being ripped from their family.

In retrospect, boarding the ship alone endangered their family. As her anxiety and self-condemnation spiraled, her heart raced faster, a threat to her baby. She cast the reproach aside and focused on Autumn. For a change, she sat and listened quietly to her sister-in-law's wisdom on child-raising, afraid her voice would give away her struggles or induce more spasms. Her pain had pretty much dissipated when Cael returned, but without Wes by his side, she doubted her troubles would be over.

"Anything?" she implored.

He shook his head and sat down beside her. "I'm at a loss on what to do. We've been at sea all day, so we can't claim he may still be on the island. Plus, how can we trust anybody to give us true answers?"

"Can't you just follow through and have them page Wes to come to the cabin?" Autumn suggested. "People have been doing that the whole week with their family members. It won't stand out as suspicious. Besides, if on the off chance nothing nefarious is unfolding, he could make his way back here. "

The detectives accepted her point and decided to make the call to the concierge desk. The announcement rang out seconds after Cael hung up, commencing their wait. Ten minutes rolled into twenty, twenty to an hour, and so on. Before long, it was dinnertime, but none of them had an appetite.

"We have to eat, and if we don't go now, we won't be able to until after the late diners are finished," Cael reminded the ladies.

"I probably won't be hungry even then," Minka said.

"But Peyton will be," he counseled her. "This is bigger than you."

"I'm not too big on how that sounds," she said.

He apologized with a grin. "I also think it's a good idea to proceed with our evening as normal. I don't mean to cause any more alarm, but Franklin may have eyes on us. The least affected we portray ourselves to be by this, the less power they have over us. It's basic negotiating skills."

Equipped with the same training and life experience as he, Minka couldn't dispute Cael's reasoning. Still, she wished she could stay behind, hating to pretend everything was fine when it wasn't. "What if Wes comes while we're gone?"

"He knows our schedule and would find us," Cael assured her, but his voice held out no promise.

She couldn't blame him for any underlying cynicism since she, too, was fighting her own. Strategies aside, her conscience badgered her about betraying her husband with her fanciful dining, all while he could be suffering—or worse—at criminals' hands. Again, remorse overwhelmed her, but for her baby's well-being, she willed her frazzled brain to dismiss it and follow Cael and Autumn to dinner.

One advantage to going to the dining room, she reckoned, was observing whether or not Stewart and Tula would make an appearance. Ever since she'd witnessed Riggs emerge from their suite with the stuffed envelope, she'd been desperate to determine what it meant for the couple. In theory, if they met the demands, they should be free of further extortion tactics, but one could never be certain. The blackmailers could abuse their control for as long as they had it. Besides, if they had used biochemical methods against Tula, she might not yet be fully recovered.

Thus, Minka didn't expect to see either of them. To her disbelief, it saddened her…but it wasn't for her social needs. To fill those, the Garrets were again the first ones at their table, with Griffin eager for his final banquet of the voyage. Janine, of course, inquired about Wes, and as planned, Minka expressed that he was simply exhausted.

"I was too beat to eat once," Griffin said, and they all waited for the inevitable punchline. He didn't disappoint. "I was under anesthesia, having an appendectomy!"

The gang played along with the joviality, but inside, Minka wondered if the couple would figure out that more lay behind Wes's absence than being tired. She doubted it since they weren't familiar with his habits, and it had been a busy week. When they began considering what detained Stewart and Tula, however, she flinched, invoking a stern glower from Cael.

It turned out to be just the five of them for the entire

meal, and Minka managed to get down most of her roasted turkey. When their waiter served dessert, she uncharacteristically declined, but the server insisted she take it.

"We always give our babymooners a special treat on their last night," she explained, setting down the lidded platter.

"Where's mine?" Griffin demanded.

Minka had to smile, lifting the lid to find a cupcake with pink and blue sprinkles along with a bib that read *Future Cruiser*. Chuckling over the clever gift, she picked up the congratulatory card, anticipating a generic message, but the very personal note shook her to her core.

You're a better sleuth than you are a wife or mother. If you want your bundle of joy to have a father, stop digging into our business, and he'll be waiting for you at the boarding center tomorrow.

Chapter Twelve

Minka excused herself from the dinner table and retreated to the restroom, where she stared at her reflection in the mirror for far too long. Gazing for answers no one could tell her, she was at a crossroads yet again between doing right by her job and right by her family. It was a quandary she'd faced both when Wes entered WITSEC, then later when her brother Robin was entangled with the law. Even so, the position flummoxed her as much as ever before.

Just like then, she had others to consider on either side. She'd taken an oath to protect her community, and it was likely Franklin's team had already undermined that. Not only did Logan Baris deserve justice, but their other victims—past, present, and future—did, as well. Turning a blind eye to their criminal acts for her husband's safety would mean denying them that, jeopardizing untold lives, and retracting her own vow. She took another vow she held precious, however, and that was, of course, her marriage vow.

From her wedding day forward, she'd done her best to care for the needs of Wes and her family, even stepping aside from the career she fought so hard for to raise their daughter. That same little girl, along with the baby she was carrying, needed a father. With all of the crime on the earth, it was hard not to question whether apprehending one or two criminals would impact the world as much as it'd affect her children to lose their dad.

Remembering Griffin's words about working in Narcotics, Minka realized it wasn't a fair comparison. Their victims were somebody's children, siblings, spouses, and parents, so she didn't have the right to decide that her family outweighed theirs. Extracting the note she concealed in her purse, she reread the menacing threat several times over, until a sudden voice jolted her from her meditating.

"Nice surprise, huh?" the woman commented in what Minka initially took to be a maniacal way. When she faced the fellow expectant mother, she realized the remark was innocent. "We deserve a little something after a week of squeezing through these tight hallways. Isn't the bib adorable?"

"It is," she agreed, having nearly forgotten about the enclosed gift.

"I could've used two, but I guess a cheap line like this can't spring for multiples. The girls will have to share."

She introduced herself as Danica and babbled on, revealing that her twins were due in December and that it was her first pregnancy. Other than asking how far along Minka was and her baby's gender, she held the entire conversation, even detailing her upcoming baby shower and her reserved delivery suite in the hospital. Minka's rumination drowned out the valley girl, making her merely nod and smile at the mom-to-be's every exclamation. Nonetheless, she appreciated it when Autumn entered the room and saved her.

"Is everything okay?" she questioned Minka. "We were worried."

"Yes, it's fantastic," Danica replied. "We've just

been jawing, mommy-to-mommy, comparing notes."

Minka was amused that she viewed their exchange to be two-sided, but she didn't bother correcting her. Rather, she wished her the best and accompanied Autumn out the door. Cael awaited them and inquired why Minka had taken so long. With the card still in her hand, she debated whether or not to divulge it then, but observing how many people surrounded them, she opted to hold off.

She resorted to humor to compensate for her dishonesty. "I was waylaid by a trophy wife, who couldn't decide whether to have a diamond-themed baby shower in Beverly Hills or a Victorian-inspired one in Europe."

Returning to their table to retrieve the bib along with Autumn's light jacket, they said their farewells to the Garrets, in case they missed one another in the morning. While they made brief small talk in closing, Minka again contemplated enlisting Griffin's help, given his experience and his close proximity to Tula and Stewart's cabin. She was continuing to compare the pros and cons when the moment ended and they parted ways.

Once the three wandered away from the big crowd, Cael asked for the women's input. "Any ideas on how to spend our evening?"

"I won't govern yours, but mine will be spent in my room," Minka told them. "I'm pregnant, tired, and I need to pack. I was planning a laidback night even before this happened."

He seemed surprised by her apathy. "What about Wes?"

She took a moment to consider her options, but she quickly concluded she only had one. Drawing them away from the cluster of passengers nearby, she showed him the note. "This came on my dessert tray."

"Guess we can rule this out as random," he stated, allowing Autumn to read it. With glazed eyes, he stood silently, rubbing his face. "Our waitress gave this to you, correct?"

Minka nodded. "I don't think she's involved, though, do you?"

"I doubt it, but we need to find out who's responsible for putting these together."

She pictured Franklin writing the threat with a sneer across his lips. "I have a feeling I already know."

They circled back to the dining room and found a busboy cleaning their table in preparation for the later guests. To their relief, their server stood off to the side with a couple of others, and the three approached her without hesitation.

Not wanting to show the devious note, Minka fought her anger and continued to play the same part she had all week. "I just wanted to express how touched I was by the gift and sweet card. It really topped off our babymoon perfectly."

"They're a big hit," their server acknowledged.

"I'm sure. Baby gear and chocolate are never far from a pregnant lady's mind," she joked in an effort not to make her transition so abrupt. "Add in a sentimental card, and you've made our day. Who composes the messages?"

The servers swapped perplexed looks before she blushed. "They're all printed with the same one."

Humiliated and infuriated, Minka was still reluctant to hand over hers to prove it was handwritten, so she just tried to recover. "Oh, wow. The font's very realistic, and maybe my hormones are romanticizing everything. Well, I just wanted to convey my appreciation to whoever put it all together. That would be you, I assume?"

"No, one of the kitchen hands. I'm not sure who handled it tonight, but I'll pass along your gratitude."

The statement was clearly a dismissal, with no room for persuading her to take them along. Hence, they shuffled away, disappointed and embarrassed.

"That was award-worthy acting," Cael remarked.

"Excuse me, but my criminal justice class conflicted with drama club."

"It isn't your fault, Minks. This just isn't going our way."

"Understatement of the year," she mumbled.

As they ambled out of the dining room, she glanced toward the twenty-four-hour buffet around the corner. Despite her stress, she had to chuckle as Griffin studied it once more, with Janine corralling him away. At the other side of the buffet, Wynn refilled a tin of fruit salad, a mundane task that sent Minka into a tailspin.

Her feet glued to the marble floor, she tugged at Cael's sleeve and mustered up her courage. "I don't think Franklin wrote the note, but I just realized who did."

"Who?"

"Logan's roommate, Wynn McCallum."

"How would he know we're here?"

"Because I told him."

Cael's shocked eyes bored into hers. "Minks, I told you not—"

"I know, but it was so awkward. The morning I was on bedrest, he brought in my breakfast, and..." Her words trailed off, as the truth uncloaked itself.

"And what?" he commanded.

"I admitted we were here investigating what happened to Logan."

"How could you?"

"You thought he was innocent, too," Minka told her disapproving partner. "Since he works in the kitchen, he could've easily written out that card."

"Guys, keep it together," Autumn admonished. "Arguing won't accomplish anything. If he's involved, shouldn't we tail him and see if he leads us to Wes?"

With the next diners trickling in for the later meal, Cael gestured to them. "I think we can assume he'll be in the kitchen for a few more hours."

His gruff rebuttal sparked a plot in Minka's brain, but she tried to mask it. "Our hands are tied, and nobody's to blame but me. Like I said, I'm going to bed. I'd just like to be alone."

Neither one made a reply, allowing her to head to the elevator alone. She hoped they wouldn't notice that she didn't order it to go to their floor.

****

Finding the ship's lower level much like it was during hers and Cael's first visit, Minka retraced their steps to the cabin Logan and Wynn once shared. She dodged several workers along the way, given the floor was exclusively for the crew. She considered it odd that it didn't have the security measures the seventh story had but selfishly rejoiced over the fact that they didn't pamper their staff as well as they did their customers.

Recalling the exact room number, Minka located it with no problem, but upon closing in on it, her suppressed fear became manifest. Because of the cruise line's restrictions, they'd had to abandon their weapons

219

back in Orlando, a hazard they should've discussed in greater detail. She surveyed the corridor for anything she could use to defend herself, having to settle for a life jacket that was hanging on the wall. With the memory fresh in mind of barely being able to fit in one four days prior, she swallowed hard that she was now employing it to keep her and her baby safe.

Holding it in one hand, she approached the door and knocked gently, in order not to alert Wynn's neighbors. Not to her surprise, no one answered, so she clutched the knob and smiled when it twisted. Figuring the occupant was busy in the kitchen like Cael presumed, Minka stepped inside and closed the door behind her. Everything appeared similar to how it did the week before, with the exception of Logan's side being empty. One possession of his remained on the nightstand between the beds.

A classic comic book.

Still in its original packaging, she picked it up gingerly and gazed at it, aware its presence confirmed the worst. Wynn was involved with Franklin and had tricked her of his innocence. She'd trusted him, a mistake that led them to this very moment.

Chiding her flawed instincts, she was too preoccupied to hear the door softly open, and the cadence of her betrayer's voice startled her. "I held one back for Luca. It was their father's collection, after all."

"How sentimental of you. Where was that loyalty when you killed his brother?"

"I didn't kill Logan. I couldn't have. That's why they didn't tell me beforehand. I just assumed we'd keep his comics until he regained his senses. I was truly devastated when I learned otherwise."

"Who are they?" Minka questioned.

"I don't think you need me to tell you, Detective. I have to admit you're quite perceptive and relentless. I was shocked when I found you here. Orlando's a safer place with you on the force."

"Obviously, not safe enough to allow psychos like you and your buddies to poison an innocent man."

Wynn snickered. "Logan was a lot of things, but he wasn't innocent. He coerced me into this. He said we deserved more than this, and our spoiled rich guests deserved less."

"So you what? Poison them until they pay you off?"

"I'll give you a sneak peek."

After scrolling through his phone—which based on the color, was different from the one he handed them on their first visit—he offered it to her. Her whole body trembled the moment she beheld Wes lying in an empty room, appearing to be unconscious.

Tears welled up in her eyes. "How much do you expect a teacher and a cop to be able to fork over?"

He chuckled. "You're a long way from the seventh floor, so believe me, money isn't our motivation here. But you can offer us something better: freedom to carry on our business without interference. As your card outlined, keep your mouth shut, and your baby daddy can walk off the ship with you tomorrow. Otherwise, he'll fall overboard."

He scooted her toward the door, as the superhero monikers tumbled into her mind. "You all seem to believe you're the victims in this, robbed of your big breaks. Logan even labeled you as heroes, but you're not. No matter what disappointments led you to this insane game of sabotage, you're the villains."

Wynn maintained his contemptuous demeanor. "We all have fantasies about ourselves, like how you burst down here, armed with a life vest that won't even fit around you."

****

Minka stormed into her cabin and slammed the door, reeling from the infuriating encounter with the traitor. Having the truth veiled from her always agitated her, but for a change, she deemed it worse to sit with the whole story unfurled in front of her. Overtaken by a mixture of terror, exasperation, and hopelessness, she sprawled out on the bed, unable to imagine sleeping on it with the visual of her husband suffering.

Aware of her blood pressure skyrocketing, she focused on her breathing and stroked her tummy. After a moment, she grabbed her tablet beside her to check the time, which showed seven o'nine. Wes had been missing for over three hours, and they wouldn't be docking for fourteen more. If he wasn't just sedated in the photo Wynn showed her, what kind of condition would he be in by morning? She kept in mind that they'd better ensure his safety if they wanted hers and Cael's cooperation. Considering Tula couldn't make an appearance at dinner even after Stewart paid up, however, she didn't put much stock in the criminals' expediency to liberate their victims.

A notification from her pregnancy app gave her a brief respite from the mayhem, as it congratulated her on hitting the twenty-three-week mark. It informed her that the baby had grown from the size of a spaghetti squash to that of a large mango and said the little one could now hear their voices.

With a smirk, she bent her head toward her middle.

"Well, Peyton, if you've been tuned in on all of this, you've already figured out what kind of mad family you have." When her words won her a flutter of movement, she continued, "I promise we'll find Daddy."

Somebody tapped on the door. In view of how many people with bad intentions knew her, she hesitated to answer it until Cael announced that it was him.

She swung it open. "Please spare me the lecture. I guess the baby can hear us now, and I don't want him or her to get the impression that I'm the senseless one in the bunch. My brother and yours share that honor."

He lowered his gaze in a contrite manner. "I'm sorry I lost my temper. I really understand why you trusted Wynn."

"Thank you."

He nodded and paused. "It just occurred to me that we narrowed down that a reporter must've been involved with Logan, as his superhero aliases suggest. I reasoned that could be Franklin since he was listed as writing up the activities pamphlet, but now, I wonder if that could be Wynn. Mind if I use your tablet."

"Sure." She lent it to him. "But I know he's part of this, given he confessed to me when I confronted him in his cabin."

He threw up his hands. "You what?'

She detailed their run-in and all that it revealed, including the image of Wes. Her brother-in-law paced then sat, before he stood and fidgeted. After she finished, she asked him, "Do you think we should give in and wait this out for the rest of the trip?"

"Not yet," he refused, his expression steely. "We need to get in touch with Gus."

He first tried to place a video call on Minka's tablet,

like they did earlier with Jaclyn and the kids. Without him signed into the app, however, they couldn't reach him. They debated emailing him to instruct him to be ready for their call, but they didn't have time to spare. With no other option, she strode over to the landline—or more fittingly, the ocean-line—on the dresser, disregarding the note that stated the ridiculous fee they'd be charged per minute.

She handed it off to Cael, whose hands were as shaky as hers. He dialed and waited for their captain to answer. Since it was around the kids' bedtime, there was no guarantee of him hearing the call over little Kennedy's nightly scream fest. He eventually picked up, but in the background, Minka could hear the ten-month-old's cries. When they started to fade away, she surmised that he'd locked himself in his quiet office. He muttered statements of astonishment over the day's turn of events.

When Minka and Cael asked for his guidance on how to handle the situation, he remained silent at first, but he soon overcame his despondency. *"If there's a silver lining to this, it's the fact that you have enough to get a search warrant executed. I'll update Brevard County, and if nothing else, they should be ready to intercept them as soon as you guys dock tomorrow."*

"But what about Wes?" Minka replied. "I can't twiddle my thumbs while they might be rendering him paralyzed. We haven't laid eyes on the poor woman they terrorized this afternoon."

"Did he appear to be in an average cabin?" Gus inquired.

"It was odd. I think he was lying on a cot, but the whole space was pretty bare. Nothing was furnished. It reminded me of a construction area."

Cael's eyes lit up. "I heard some staff saying one of the floors is under construction. I think they said it's the eighth one."

"That would make sense, considering they target the rich people on the seventh floor," Minka replied. "But how could they get away with anything around a construction crew?"

"From what I gathered, it's been out of commission for a while now," Cael said. "The cruise-line may not have the budget to complete it, or maybe Franklin is delaying it on his end to keep it for their schemes."

"Are there any security guards or somebody you guys can trust to help you pursue this?" Gus asked.

She snorted. "I thought there was, but that's what landed us here."

Gus sighed. *"I realize it's dicey but allowing them to hold Wes there all night may be riskier still."*

Before their conversation concluded, the captain said he'd alert the Coast Guard and determine if they could somehow assist. With them unable to provide their current coordinates, though, it'd be a feat to garner their help, much less at the rapid pace they needed it. As they hung up, Minka's hopes sank to the ocean floor. Cael leveled the very expression she expected at her, the one that conveyed *I know you won't like this, but we have to do it*.

She cut him off before he had a chance to utter the words. "No, we are not involving Shantelle."

"But we have an in with her. She confessed her love for Logan out of nowhere to you. You weren't cornering her into giving you that as a defense. I think we can trust her this time."

"That's what your brother assumed last time,

remember? Sure, she might love Logan, but she also loved that mobster and was willing to kill for him. She'd be in an even better position to kill Wes now than she was then." A glance at the clock led her to a convenient realization. "Besides, she's performing right now."

He didn't dispute that. "It'd be challenging to flag anyone down on a busy night like this."

She nodded before an idea struck her. "Instead of a crew member, maybe we just need a back-up detective."

Cael grinned and rose to his feet. "Okay, you win."

****

Minka and Cael couldn't be definitive about Griffin and Janine's present whereabouts, but they agreed to start in their cabin. At dinner, Janine talked about having to pack up and their need for a good night's rest before their busy day of travelling. Minka hated to intrude on that, but even after being acquainted with them for such a short time, she sensed that they would want to help if they were in a position to.

Thus, they took a chance on breaching the seventh floor. As they'd hoped, no security guards had a post by the little-used stairwell, allowing them to quietly thread into the crowd. With the entry not far from the Garrets' cabin, Cael drummed on the door. Minka's gaze slid to the Hawkings' room, but it remained quiet over there. Before long, Griffin responded with a concerned Janine behind his shoulder.

"We're sorry to interrupt your evening, guys," Cael told them. "We're in a tight spot, though, and could use some input from a fellow LEO."

"Sure. I'll let you consult with Janine, and I'll wait on the balcony," Griffin joked.

Minka and Cael strode inside the luxurious room

and took a seat on the plush sofa. Janine busied herself with packing her suitcase in the bedroom portion to grant them privacy, although the partial wall between the spaces allowed her to hear everything. As the partners took turns summarizing their mission on *The Exquisite Marvel*, Griffin manifested more and more of his official persona, while Janine kept pausing her motions. By the end, she abandoned her efforts and joined them in the impromptu Situation Room.

Griffin shook his head after they finished their narrative. "Do you really believe those fools would take the chance of carting bioweapons onto a ship? If any of it leaked through the vents, the whole vessel would be contaminated."

"We're not certain of anything," Cael admitted. "Given Cromwell's history with Tabun and the fact that it likely killed our victim, we're zeroing in on it being a real possibility."

"I just can't convince myself that the photo of Wes is a bluff," Minka said. "They could toss him overboard and flee the ship before us tomorrow, and we'd never recover him."

"I understand your fears, honey, but try not to let your imagination run too wild, for your child's sake," Janine admonished.

Minka expressed her appreciation before Griffin continued to strategize. "You said Tula and Stewart were targeted?"

Cael nodded. "We're pretty confident of that."

"Let's pay them a visit and try to pump them for details."

Minka didn't have high hopes of them cooperating, of the opinion the criminals would've bound them to secrecy. Then again, what leverage did they retain over their victims once they were paid off and returned them? Did they keep the passengers in their lair until the end of the ship's voyage, like Wynn claimed to let her reunite with Wes at the boarding station?

The trio shuffled down the hall, with Griffin at the lead. Stewart didn't answer his first two knocks, but he gave in on the third. He still wore his exhaustion, with rings circling his weary eyes. Even so, he maintained his pompous demeanor. "May I help you?"

"We believe you can, Mr. Hawkings. May we come in?" Griffin asked.

"I'm sorry, but my wife is still under the weather."

"Perhaps you could join us in our suite," Griffin offered.

Minka opted to appeal to the man's ego. "We need your expertise in a federal offense."

Stewart's constant grimace faded a notch, and he acquiesced. Once behind closed doors, Cael jumped to the chase. "We're aware Tula was taken because her abductors took my brother, too."

His expression remained cryptic. "I'm not following you."

Her little tolerance of the guy already toast, Minka demanded, "In that case, I'd like to see her."

Stewart lowered his head. "If I say anything, they might hurt her further. You face the same with your husband."

Griffin pounced on the indirect confession. "They still have her, then?"

Stewart peeked around both shoulders, clearly distrustful of the room's security. At last, he bobbed his head in affirmation.

"Did they indicate where they're keeping her?" Cael inquired.

He shook his head.

"Did they show you a picture?" Minka asked.

Through nonverbal communication, they learned his experience mirrored Minka's, with Tula appearing to be in a room under renovation. He gave them one more tidbit, whispering, "After I paid them, they gave her an antidote and permitted me to talk to her over a walkie-talkie. She sounded groggy, and they told me she needs two more injections of it to make a full recovery. From my time with the Bureau, I can attest to that."

Still unsure of his credibility, Minka weighed how much they could believe, but short on resources, they had to accept it. Cael stated, "Sounds like I need to go upstairs. Minks, you stay put. We can't endanger the baby."

"I agree, but I won't let you go alone. If you're exposed and pass out, they'll have both of you."

An awkward silence ensued, as neither guy hastened to volunteer. Minka understood their reluctance, with Griffin just entering retirement and no doubt still exhaling from surviving his dangerous career. Obviously, Stewart wouldn't want to incense the crooks further for his wife's sake, but given the FBI career he touted, she wanted to challenge him to use his supposed training. She restrained her crafty impulses, with it being no time for mind games.

Cael cut the tension by standing up. "I'll be fine."

His partner wouldn't accept it. "These floors are huge. I can go with you and stay out of wherever they're conducting this charade. At least I could stand guard and discern if you need help."

"How can we know where you'd be safe? They could have the level full of victims."

"I doubt they'd be that bold. Someone could always wander up there, so they'd probably set it up away from the entrance. Besides, they wouldn't want to give their victims easy access to an escape route," she told Cael.

"I agree with her," Griffin said. "I'll tag along with her and assist if I can."

Cael accepted the strategy, and they took the stairs up to the next floor. A rope across the doorway restricted access to guests due to the remodel, but they simply unfastened it from its post. Cael selected a fire extinguisher on the wall to be his weapon, and Griffin grabbed a crowbar lying on the floor from the few renovation efforts that had taken place. Along their trek, Minka picked up a nail gun from the floor, evoking one last "Check you out!" from Griffin. She called to mind the instruction Wes gave her on using it in the nursery, baffled she'd have such an opportunity to test her skills.

Not hearing any movement, they peered in several different directions until a voice echoed from the north corridor. All of the doors in the hall stood open—except for the one at the end. Cael padded that way, throwing back a finger at Minka to command her to follow her own plan. Griffin halted his steps beside her, reinforcing the agreed approach.

As Cael vanished from her view, uncertainty filled Minka, given the unusual circumstances. Their badges carried no authority in the international waters, so he was facing the enemies as no more than a vigilante. All of the holes in her idea to board the ship ripped through her brain before a cough in the distance stole her attention. Resounding from the south side, it carried her husband's tone. Without hesitation, her anxious feet whisked her toward the noise, and she ignored Griffin's appeals to stop.

Her harried journey ended at a room with a large circular window, similar to the ones she'd spotted on other levels that contained vending machines. A cot occupied this one, with Wes atop it. Though she was elated to observe him awake, his continued coughing unnerved her.

She took a step closer, but Griffin grasped her shoulder. "You can't."

Since the area didn't have a door, she figured he'd be able to hear her. "Wes, we're here!"

He swung his head toward her. "Honey?"

"We have to track down Cael," she told Griffin.

He didn't protest, jogging back that way. Before they made it very far, Franklin rounded a corner, holding a gun to Cael. "Why couldn't you just wait at the boarding station for your husband, like we told you to?"

"Why couldn't you just let Logan out of this operation of yours instead of poisoning him?" Minka asked.

Franklin sneered. "He gave himself the Tabun. He wanted to get sick and go into the hospital so he could rat us all out."

Now the haphazard circumstances made sense to her. "You intercepted him before he made it and shot him once the Tabun killed him?"

"Just like I can shoot your partner here."

With Cael having lost his fire extinguisher somewhere along the line, she and Griffin retained the only makeshift weapons, neither of which rivaled the revolver. Formulating their best defense, Minka's attention deviated to another nasty cough from Wes. Her gaze drifted toward the alcove where he lay when she spotted the nearby fire alarm. In that instant, she devised her plan.

She yanked on the lever, causing the piercing distress signal to bellow through the entire vessel. Taken aback, Franklin loosened his grip on Cael, who elbowed him and knocked his gun from his hand. The detective recovered it as Griffin struck Franklin with the crowbar, hurling him to the ground.

Minka dashed back toward Wes, but Riggs suddenly appeared and bolted for her. As he grabbed her arm, she drove the nail gun into his side and fired it. He winced, then let out a yelp of pain. Freed, she sent another nail into his arm. She realized they wouldn't put him out of commission for long, so she rushed away.

After he overcame the element of surprise, he chased her straight to the stairwell, where the ship's emergency squad had just arrived.

"Guys, you have to help us restrain these unruly passengers," Riggs told his crewmates.

Shantelle emerged from the center of the cluster. "I don't think they're the problem here."

At the first mate's command, they apprehended the criminals. He proceeded to inform the detectives that the Coast Guard had alerted the command station of Gus's distress call.

Once the commotion abated, Minka sped into the area where Wes remained on the cot, but she stopped short, afraid of the danger he posed to her and Peyton. "Did Cromwell ever administer the antidote to you?"

Wes grinned. "He didn't give me anything but a dose of anesthesia."

"What caused all of your hacking, then?"

"High school drama class, same as Autumn."

She chuckled and scrambled inside to cut off the zip-ties that fastened his ankles to the cot. Once she did so, she embraced him.

After they kissed, he teased her, "Now, do you believe Shantelle has changed?"

Epilogue

Four Months Later

Seated at her desk, Minka ran through everything she needed to accomplish before her maternity leave began. Though she wasn't due for ten days, Dr. Bailey informed her at her check-up yesterday that the baby could arrive any day. After consulting with Gus, she decided to finish out the week if Peyton allowed and take it easy for however long she could.

As she organized her files, a visitor entered the precinct and stole everyone's attention. Sadie beamed at the officers who swarmed around her and her two-week-old daughter, Daphne. Minka remained in her chair, uneager to fight the crowd, and waited for the new mom to wander over. Once they all satisfied their urge to coo over the infant, Sadie strolled over with the carrier and displayed her to Minka.

Minka gently stroked Daphne's cheek as she slept through the adults' fussing. "She has really grown since we visited last week."

"I know! I can't get over how much she changes every day. My mom offered to take her during my interview with the DA, but I couldn't bear to leave her. I can already tell these next ten weeks will fly by, so I want to soak up every minute I can."

"I don't blame you. Was your interview about

Logan's murder?"

Sadie nodded. "They want as many details as they can get before the trial starts."

"Wes and I have an appointment there on Friday, baby-permitting. Considering what's emerged, they have a pretty solid case."

In the months since the cruise's end, many more details had surfaced about the crewmates' exploits. The accompanying media coverage prompted other victims to reveal the experiences they'd been too afraid to share. A total of thirty-six reported their accounts to the authorities and were testifying against the criminals in a federal case. In advance of that, Orlando charged them with Logan's murder, fortunately their only one.

They'd also uncovered a lot about the murder victim and his own part in the extortion operation, revealing how vital of a role he played. His cohorts gladly exposed his duties of getting acquainted with their marks before handing them over to be poisoned. Through it all, his brother, Luca, cooperated and stayed in touch with her and Cael, and in an ironic twist, Shantelle did, too. In fact, the two had found solace in each other and began dating.

Sadie motioned toward the framed photo of one of her and Wes's poses on the cruise ship, taken by Riggs. "It cracks me up that you still display those pictures, even after the photographer almost killed you guys."

"Why shouldn't I? They're gorgeous. At this point, I need a reminder of what my feet look like, especially in beautiful heels." She winked. "Besides, it reminds me of my satisfaction of shooting that nail into his arm."

Sadie laughed just before Daphne started to cry, signaling that her mom better take her home. The conversation prompted Minka to print off some of the notes she'd compiled about the case for their upcoming meeting with the district attorney's office. Throughout the course of the afternoon, however, she developed a hunch that they'd have to reschedule, as jabs pierced through Minka's back and stomach. With each one becoming increasingly sharp and more frequent, she didn't have difficultly figuring out what they meant.

By the end of their shift, her contractions were spaced just shy of five minutes apart. She told Cael, "I think we'd better make a pit-stop at the maternity ward."

****

With Minka's labor progressing faster than it had the first time, Dr. Bailey instructed her to push before four hours passed. Holding her hand, Wes coached his wife through the pain of childbirth once again. After her third push, a cry echoed through the room, after which the doctor presented their newborn.

She made the all-important announcement. "It's a boy!"

"A boy?" Wes cried out in confusion.

"Isn't that what you kept implying to me?" Minka asked.

"Yes, but that's because I was trying to fool you! Dr. Bailey showed me a girl."

"That's what she told you, anyhow," Minka replied.

"I told him the truth, Minka. It was a girl, but it was the sonogram of my daughter three years ago. I would've fibbed if needed, though," she explained with a smirk. "Your wife was a step ahead of you."

Minka beamed. "I wanted us both to be surprised."

He had to kiss her, and she giggled, realizing once more what a perfect match they were. The doctor handed

Minka their little son, who instantly filled a gap his mother didn't realize she had, like his sister did seven years prior. After the nurse whisked him away to clean him up, Wes ushered Caela in, who was oblivious to the surprise they had in store.

Minka held her breath, nervous for the way she'd react to not having a sister. She released a sigh of relief—and a slight chuckle—when her daughter rejoiced. "I don't have to share my toys!"

Her dad gently corrected her, but Minka stroked his arm, not wanting anything to taint their first moments as a family of four. Astonishment continued to be the theme for the next couple of days, with their friends and family all expecting to welcome another baby girl at the hospital. Of course, the initial shock didn't rob their shared joy and excitement over the little boy's arrival into their lives.

"Two grandsons, and one on the way," Wes and Cael's father, Bill, marveled, holding Peyton.

Autumn and Cael, in the process of adopting a five-month-old from Thailand, beamed. Because the polyps on her uterus proved to be precancerous, Autumn was undergoing hormone treatment that restricted them from conceiving for three more years. Uneager to wait that long to give Tyson a sibling, they started the adoption process and were ecstatic when the agency notified them about baby Kamon—meaning "from the heart"—a month ago. They hoped to be able to complete the paperwork and travel there by year's end.

"The department's going to be shorthanded if their star detectives are both on parental leave," Jaclyn said.

"Nah, our new interim detective, Griffin, has us covered," Cael replied.

1

"As long as Gus feeds him well!" Minka added.

A week after Minka and Peyton returned home from the hospital, both sides of the family and the Channings gathered to celebrate. As she observed the people she loved talk and laugh together, Minka wondered what she'd done to deserve such a full life. Remembering the disappointments that led Franklin and his accomplices to crime, she realized that they weren't alone in their misery.

At several points in her own life, she almost joined them in their bitterness, convinced she was doomed to exist in silence, void of love or happiness. Yet, twists that she couldn't have imagined propelled her to this beautiful, loud moment. Despite the many obstacles she faced over time, she relied on her strong spirit, wit, and the love she shared with others to remain undefeated.

A word about the author...

Karina Bartow grew up and still lives in Northern Ohio. Though born with Cerebral Palsy, she's never allowed her disability to define her. Rather, she's used her experiences to breathe life into characters who have physical limitations, but like her, are determined not to let them stand in the way of the life they want. Along with the Unde(a)feated Detective Series, her works include "Wrong Line, Right Connection" and "Forgetting My Way Back to You". She may only be able to type with one hand, but she writes with her whole heart! http://www.karinabartow.com

Thank you for purchasing
this publication of The Wild Rose Press, Inc.

For questions or more information
contact us at
info@thewildrosepress.com.

The Wild Rose Press, Inc.
www.thewildrosepress.com